MW01275655

MOWED OVER

Sonoma Book 2

Mae Harden

II

This is a work of fiction. Names, characters, businesses, places, events, locales, and incidents are either the products of the author's imagination or used in a fictitious manner. Any resemblance to actual persons, living or dead, or actual events is purely coincidental.

Cover art Copyright © 2020 by Mae Harden

Editing by Kraken Communications

Copyright © 2020 by Mae Harden

All rights reserved. This book or any portion thereof may not be reproduced or used in any manner whatsoever without the express written permission of the author except for the use of brief quotations in a book review.

Printed in the United States of America

First Printing, 2020

www.maeharden.com

IV

Dedicated to my girlfriends Emily, Becky, Brittany, and Stacey for their unending support and to Juniper, who pushes me to work harder, faster, and better.

A note from the author

I know trigger warnings are a controversial topic within the romance community. I'm a reader too, and I can't tell you how many debates I've seen on this topic. If you don't have triggers and don't want to read any warnings, jump your cute butt on over to Chapter 1. Go on! Dive in and enjoy!

If you're sticking around and reading this, I'm giving you one last chance to avoid a spoiler. You cool?

Okay, here's your trigger warning: there's a stalker in this book. I'm fairly certain you read the description and understood that was going to happen, but I don't want this sneaking up on anyone that might find it upsetting. I have my own triggers and I know from personal experience how painful it can be to have them sprung on you. I never want someone to go through that because of my work.

My dear readers, I love you. I hope you love Lilah and Ben as much as I do, but if stalkers are a hard limit, skip this book and come back for Lukas' story. He's got a major bad boy thing going on: tattoos, a motorcycle, and a chip on his shoulder. Plus, the sex in that book is crazy hot. Just saying. You'll love it.

Sincerely,

Mae

Chapter 1: Ben

There's a rumble outside and I look over my steaming cup of coffee to peer out the kitchen window. I watch as a short, curvy woman wearing big sunglasses and two big dudes climb out of a rented moving truck. Looks like the new neighbor is finally moving in. The house was only on the market for a few days before someone snapped it up. Gossip around the neighborhood is that a single woman bought it, no kids.

Despite the size differences between the moving trio, I'm sure those guys are Short Stack's brothers. They've all got the same inky hair and tan skin. Plus, it looks like one of them is giving her a hard time and she just shoved him in the chest with all her might. He didn't move an inch, just looked at her like she was a tiny, exasperating puppy. The sight makes me laugh and I accidentally snort my scorching hot coffee, scalding my sinuses.

An alert pings on my watch. As entertaining as snooping on the new neighbor is, it's time to get to work. I plop down in my desk chair and crack my knuckles as my computer wakes up. I double check my security feeds and my yard sensors. They've never been set off by anything more threatening than a family of raccoons and that asshole, Mr. Miller, who likes to let his dog poop in my yard. Still, better safe than sorry.

I lose myself in work for a couple hours and I'm just making sure I didn't leave any digital breadcrumbs when my phone buzzes on my desk. My best friend's name shows on the screen. I hate talking on the phone, so I ignore him, but Jack's never been good at taking a hint and the phone buzzes again. Muttering to myself, I answer it. Only because I know he won't stop until I do. My best, and only, friend is stubborn as a motherfucker.

"Why can't you text like a normal person?" I ask.

I can hear the wind rushing by in the background and I'd bet money he's driving his beloved convertible with the top down. "We're going out tonight. No excuses." At least he cuts straight to the chase.

"Hard no. I'd rather stay home and have a beer."

"You need to get out of that house. I swear, you've become a hermit.

What's the point of living in Sonoma if you never go out? I'm half afraid I'll find you holed up with bottles of piss everywhere. You need a night out before you do a full Howard Hughes."

"A, that's disgusting, and I would never. B, you'd never get in my house if I didn't want you to."

"Ben, you aren't helping your case with that shit. Dude, I don't use this word often, but *please*. I've got a couple investors visiting from New York and they want to go to Blue Ruin for cocktails. I can't take a night out with these guys without moral support. They always want to go to someone else's bar when they're in town. I mean, what's the fucking point of owning a winery if I have to pay someone else to pour my drink? Whatever. Just come with us. Drinks and food are on me."

I laugh at that. "Like I need you to be my sugar daddy."

"Come on, man. I promise it won't be that bad. I'll owe you one."

Sighing inwardly, I already know I'm going to regret this. "Fuck. Fine. Fine, I'll come. But I'm getting a Lyft, I'm not bar hopping with those douchebags, and I'm not drinking anything with garnishes."

"Deal. Only the best whiskey for you, ya grumpy bastard. I promise to keep you in the lifestyle to which you've become accustomed," Jack says before hanging up on me.

***

Blue Ruin is, well, strange. We live in Sonoma, California. It's wine country at its best. Comfortable, casual, quietly sophisticated, and homey. Blue Ruin is a speakeasy-style bar that looks like somebody copied and pasted it from Brooklyn. It's packed with the Bro-iest of Bros and tourists with more money than taste, all pounding back $14 cocktails with ridiculous specialty ice cubes.

The club is dark with oversized leather booths, velvet armchairs and quirky light fixtures fitted with Edison bulbs. I can't decide if the decor would

2

be better suited for a steampunk clubhouse or a BDSM club (if you swap out the velvet for more leather, because I can only imagine how hard it would be to get cum out of velvet.) This is decidedly *not* my kind of place. I'm a computer nerd from Texas. I'd be a lot more comfortable somewhere with less... this. But I can make do as long as I can get a whiskey without egg white foam on top.

I find Jack and three of his visiting investors at a booth in the back. A server with a bow tie and a curled-up mustache is dropping off some overly complicated cocktails and, according to his spiel, the "locally sourced pickle tray." It's hard not to roll your eyes at locally sourced pickles, but I manage.

Jack and his investors talk wine for a bit. They're all laughing and having a good time. Cabernet is having a great year, I guess. Jack has been working non-stop since his father passed away a couple months ago, trying to turn his family winery around. It looks like things are finally starting to fall into place for him.

I zone out, swirling my second whisky around in its glass, lost in thought until a flash of red catches my eye.

A womanly hip bumps the kitchen door open and heads toward the bar, looking like something out of a dirty dream. She's juggling three big jars of those damn pickles, her body swaying with every step, causing her short, black skirt to ride up her tan thighs. She's wearing a sleeveless cherry red silk blouse that shows off her neck, long, slim and delicate. Her silky dark ponytail swings over her shoulder, just begging to be pulled.

Maybe she can feel me staring because she looks up and meets my eyes. My heart stutters and my breath catches in my chest. Her eyes are a startling bottle green and fuck me running if she isn't the prettiest woman I've ever seen. With her high cheekbones and cupid's bow mouth, there's something vaguely familiar about her, but I can't quite place it.

Her eyes dart away, but I didn't miss the way she looked me up and down, an edge of appreciation in her arched eyebrow. A split second later she trips on a floor mat, stumbling and dropping all three jars of pickles. Glass skitters everywhere as they smash on the tiled floor and a tiny tsunami of pickle juice floods her shoes.

3

I'm on my feet to help her before my brain catches up with my body. Her face is beet red as she squats down, carefully, in her short skirt and cleans up the glass. She waves me off as I approach, avoiding all eye contact. I stoop down to help scoop up the pickles anyway, making sure I angle my body so no one can see up her skirt. Her eyes skate over mine for just a split second, flashing with embarrassment. "You don't need to do that. I can clean this up."

"I know," I tell her with a grin. "But I'm happy to help." She meets my eyes again and gives me a brief smile. I swear to god, it's like someone flipped a switch and sucked all the air out of the room. I can barely breathe when she looks at me.

"Thank y- ouch!" A piece of glass falls from her hand. Her finger looks fine for a second, but then a bright red streak of blood spreads across the tip. Taking her elbow, I help her stand before snagging a bar napkin and wrapping it around her finger.

I'm a terrible person, because she needs a proper bandage, but I don't want to let her go. I apply pressure, loving the way her little hand feels in mine. I open my mouth. Whether I want to ask her where the first aid kit is or if I can take her out to dinner, I'm not entirely sure.

"You okay, Lilah?"

She cocks her head to the side, like a curious puppy. Fuck, she's cute. "How'd you-"

I tap my chest and grin at her. "Name tag. I'm Ben," I tell her. She looks down at her chest, and laughs. Her hand feels so soft and warm in mine. I have to remind myself that I'm trying to stop the flow of blood.

"Right. Nice to meet you, Ben. I swear I'm not usually that ditsy. The pickle fumes are getting to me and-" I don't get to hear the rest of her theory on pickle fumes though, because we're interrupted by another employee.

"How did you drop all those pickles?" He asks Lilah, stepping into her space while ignoring me completely. She visibly cringes as he gets close and it sets me on edge. Somebody doesn't understand boundaries. I eye the interloper; he's wearing suspenders over a striped shirt, and a fedora. Bold move, Cotton.

4

"Sorry, Terry," she says as she takes a step away from him. "The edge of the mat was rolled over again. I tripped. Maybe you can finally get that mat replaced now that it smells like a pickle." She smiles with false sweetness and I stifle a grin.

He eyes me like this is all my fault. "You can have a seat, sir," dismissing me and stepping between me and Lilah in one swift movement. He puts a hand on her back. "Let's get you bandaged up."

I immediately hate this guy. I have the insane urge to rip his hands off her, but Lilah brushes his arm away.

"I can take care of this myself," she tells him with a stony expression. Jesus, she's awesome. I'm liking her more and more by the second.

The guy holds up his hands and walks away muttering, "Just trying to be nice."

Lilah holds her hand up to keep the bleeding under control. "Sorry about the manager. He is the actual worst. Thanks again for the help. I'm going to go... take care of this."

"Be careful," I tell her with a grin before watching her walk away, hips swinging as she leaves pickle juice footprints in her wake. I make my way back to the table and groan inwardly when I see Jack's expression. He's got an eyebrow raised, and he's smirking.

"Friend of yours?" he asks.

"Nah." I don't make eye contact with him as I down the rest of my whiskey and flag our waiter for another.

One of Jack's investor friends, Rod (I think?) brays in an obnoxious New Jersey accent. "You got dibs, man?" I give him the most disdainful look I can muster.

"Are you five? Did you seriously just ask if I have dibs on a human being? What the fuck, Ron?"

"It's Rod, jackass," he snaps back at me. "Lighten up, bro." He runs his hands through the front of his hair, making sure it's still sticking up in front. He looks like he's got a hair horn and I hate it.

God, he has a punchable face. I give Jack my best *you-fucking-owe-me* look. Rod is just lucky I'm not a physically violent person.

Chapter 2: Lilah

Well, hell. That was embarrassing. I've been telling Terry for weeks that stupid mat keeps rolling up on one corner. We've all tripped on it at least once, but he's too cheap to deal with it. I'd be pleased about destroying it with pickle juice, but he'll probably just force one of us to hose it down out back.

What really ticks me off is that I wouldn't have even tripped if it wasn't for the hot-as-hell man sitting in the corner. I could practically feel his eyes on me when I came out of the kitchen. He looked at me like he could eat me whole.

Even now, back at his table with the winery douchebags, I can still feel him watching me through his dark-rimmed glasses. God, I love a man in glasses. He's sipping his whiskey, trying not to be obvious about it but failing catastrophically. Some of the other guys at his table are less subtle. Boy-Band Hair literally wiggled his eyebrows at me. Barf. That guy has a seriously punchable face.

I wonder why Ben is even here with those assholes. The guys in suits have cringe-worthy Jersey accents, but Ben sounds Southern and he couldn't look more different if he tried. He's wearing worn jeans and a tight gray t-shirt. His hair is sandy brown and though it's short on the sides, it's longer on top, tousled and curly. He looks so damn touchable. He holds the old-fashioned glass in his enormous hand, swirling it with the single oversized ice cube before bringing it to his full lips. I imagine what those lips would feel like on my body and I'm wracked by a full body shiver.

He seemed into me but obviously, my imagination is running wild because nothing says sexy like a clumsy woman with a bloody hand, covered in pickle juice. I'll probably never get the smell out of my shoes; I realize with a sigh. On the bright side, I bet I could market it as man repellent. Just bottle up tiny jars of cardamom sweet pickles with a label that reads "smash in case of unwanted male attention."

"How's the finger, Lilah?"

Speaking of... a voice from right behind me sends chills crawling up my spine, nearly making me drop the glass I've been wiping down. Here we fucking go again. My boss is looking me up and down, leaning back against the bar. I'd bet a hundred bucks he thinks he looks cool. Spoiler alert, it just makes him look shorter and more weaselly.

"It's fine, thanks," I say shortly, trying to make it clear I don't want to keep talking. He doesn't take the hint. *Shocker.*

"Listen," he says, pressing his thin lips together, "those pickles were really expensive--"

"Take them out of my paycheck," I tell him as I aggressively shake a gin fizz. The ice in the cocktail shaker is deafening, but that doesn't stop him. He crosses his arms and slides in closer to me.

"Oh, don't worry about it. I can cover it. I just thought maybe you would want to go out for dinner sometime."

I glare at him. "Then why would you bring up the cost of the pickles at all? Sorry, but it sounds like you, as my manager, are trying to blackmail me into a date with you because I dropped three jars of awful pickles. But that can't be right, because surely you know that would give me grounds to sue for sexual harassment."

He looks at me, mouth gaping like a dying fish. I don't know why he thought that would work. Sidestepping a still-silent Terry, I get back to work.

I don't need this shit. Literally, I don't need any of it. If the thought of using my trust fund didn't make me so insanely uncomfortable, I would walk out of here and go live on a tropical island all by myself. I could lay on the beach all damn day without a care in the world. Despite my desire to support myself without using Grandpa's money, I don't think I can take this job much longer.

Making a mental note to send the owner of the bar an email citing hostile work environments, I hand the gin fizz off to a woman wearing at least five pounds of jewelry. She clings to the man she's with as he slides me a $20 and tells me to keep the change. Out of the corner of my eye, I see Ben following the group of winery guys outside. He doesn't even look back as he steps through the door, and I shouldn't be disappointed. It's not like he owes me anything.

I take another drink order but before I can finish making it; I see a hand tap-tap-tap on the counter and I look up into the most beautiful chocolate brown eyes. The breath whooshes out of me as Ben grins at me, leaning one elbow on the bar between two women who *do not* seem to mind the way he's encroaching on their personal space. I think I just caught one of them yanking her top a little lower.

"What are you doing tomorrow?" he drawls.

"Sleeping in," I answer blissfully. "I have one day off a week and I like to use it wisely by sleeping until noon."

"Could I take you to brunch after you wake up?"

I freeze, mouth open, hanging on the precipice of something scary, because a part of me *really* wants to say yes. He seems sweet, but what do I really know about him? Nothing! He could be a super charming serial killer for all I know. He could be setting the trap with his devastating good looks and raw sex appeal.

I mean, that's not likely, is it? But my mom thought my father was a sweetheart and all it got her was a gold-digging scumbag of a husband.

"Ah... thanks for the offer, but I don't think I can," I squeak. Before my brain can catch up with my dumbass mouth, I blurt out, "but maybe another time."

Ben grins at me, unfazed, and for a second I wonder if he even heard me turn him down. "I'd like that. See you around, Lilah."

I try to ignore the way the women watch him as he taps his fingers on the bar and grins at me as he leaves. My brain is patting itself on the back for getting out of a date with Ben, but the land down under is planning a mutiny in my skirt. Tamping down my irritation, I offer the two women a free drink. Anything to distract them from watching Ben's tight rear end walk out the front door.

I'm still thinking about Ben and his glorious ass when I walk into my new home at 2am. This has been the longest damn day of my life. You'd think

I would have had the foresight to request the entire day off, but I didn't realize how exhausting moving would be. It's not like I had to move a bunch of furniture. Most of the big stuff in the apartment was my roommate's, and my brothers moved the heavy stuff for me. All I had to worry about were my clothes, some bathroom stuff, and my tortoise, Frankie.

The move still took hours longer than I thought it would, and I barely made it in for my shift this evening. And then the pickles and Ben... I showered, but I can still smell the pickles on me. I wish I smelled like Ben instead. Just the thought of him makes me wish all kinds of dirty things.

Chapter 3: Ben

I'm not a stare-at-the-ceiling-and-ponder-life kind of guy. I've never needed a ton of sleep and I get restless lying around in bed. There's too much to do. People to help, things to fix, workouts to do. You get the idea. This stupid house bothers me most. A vintage California bungalow sounds so great in theory, but there's a never-ending list of upgrades and replacements to take care of. Like the ripple in the drywall centered straight over my headboard.

For the first time since I can remember, I wake up and don't move. I open my eyes and stare at the poorly crafted ceiling, my mind working. I can't get that bartender Lilah out of my head. Not that I'm trying very hard. Images of her cleaning up broken glass in that short skirt keep creeping back in, sneaky as a fox in a henhouse. She was sexy as fuck, even with pickle juice splashed all over her. Something about the hungry look in her big green eyes is haunting me and won't let up.

Throwing an arm behind my head, I debate the merits of going back to the speakeasy tonight to see if I can get her number. She said, "maybe another time" and technically tonight is another time. It didn't feel like a complete brush-off, either. The way she blurted it out was almost hopeful, even if she looked like she wanted to take it back a second later.

I pick up a book from my nightstand on FBI interrogation tactics, but after a few minutes I toss it away again. All I can think about is Lilah. She's out there somewhere, sleeping in, and I bet she looks like a fucking angel when she sleeps. All that long, dark hair fanned across her pillow, lips parted as she breathes peacefully...

My phone buzzes on the nightstand, interrupting much more exciting thoughts. There are three people in this world who call me. Everyone else has the decency to email or a text. I doubt Jack is up after his night out with the douchebags, so that leaves my mother and my sister. The call ends and the messages start dinging. So that'll be Ella, on a burner phone most likely. I could make her wait, but she's not known to be patient when someone needs help.

About half of my work consists of legitimate consulting. Call it cyber security testing or white hat hacking. Either way, it boils down to a cushy paycheck for very little effort. Plus, it's a suitable cover for what I do the rest of the time. The thing that Ella probably needs me to do for someone right now.

The message waiting for me is a cakewalk. I don't mean to brag, but I'm amazing with computers. Okay, I mean to brag a little, but I've found the perfect way to put my skills to good use and make a decent living without ever having to set foot in a stuffy office or, perish the thought, work for the government ever again. Most of what I do isn't exactly legal. If we're being technical, it's very, very illegal. But illegal doesn't mean the same thing as unethical. The way I see it, I'm providing a necessary service and making the world a better place.

Look, if there's one thing I hate, it's a scumbag who terrorizes innocent people. And if said scumbag has his bank account wiped, his world turned inside out, and all of his dirtiest secrets made public and/or handed over to the police... well, justice has been served, hasn't it?

I'm not hugely picky on which scumbags I'll deal with. Pedophiles, stalkers, abusive boyfriends, coaches or teachers that cross the line... you've got a dirt bag the cops can't nail? I'll fix it. Occasionally, though, being a digital vigilante isn't enough. Sometimes it's safer for a woman to disappear and start a fresh life; a necessity that is almost impossible in the digital age.

Unless you have me.

Given enough time, I can hack any system on the planet. I can build a completely legitimate new identity for someone, down to a new social security number and job references. I can even hack facial recognition databases and fix it so that not even those systems will recognize my client. I say client, but I've made it a policy not to charge for that side of my work. For one thing, I don't need the money. Legitimate corporate consulting makes me more money than I could spend in a lifetime. For another, I can't have anything leading back to me or my family. I'm not an idiot. Nothing is foolproof, but 99% of the time the money trail is what gets people caught.

12

I bury myself in my work and within a couple of hours, Katie Dohner, of Colorado Springs is no more. Welcome to the world, Bridget Dixon from Tulsa. *L'chaim.*

As soon as I wrap up her new digital identification, I send it to my sister. All Bridget Dixon has to do now is order a "replacement license" from the state of Arizona and slide into her shiny new life.

Unfortunately, there's nothing left inside the house to distract me and my thoughts immediately shift back to last night at the bar. There's no point in trying to analyze my attraction for Lilah. I want to get to know her better and it's an impulse I don't think I've ever had before. The pressing need to be close to her is as unfamiliar as it is intense. I've never been one for small talk or meeting new people. I only had a few short minutes with her, but I've never been that comfortable or relaxed with anyone, and I'm going to chase that feeling.

Chapter 4: Lilah

Ben picks me up and puts me on the bar, stepping between my thighs as he kisses me, hard and full of need. His hands grip my hips as he drops down in front of me, biting and kissing the inside of my thigh. Throwing my head back on a moan, I'm distracted by the sound of a leaf blower. I try to block it out and focus on Ben talking dirty to me with his Texas twang, but the guy with the leaf blower walks right into the bar.

"Excuse me, do you mind?" I shout over the ruckus. Ben buries his head between my legs, ignoring the guy with the leaf blower. But now I've lost my concentration and no matter what kind of oral wizardry is going on downtown, I can't come when I'm distracted.

"Hey!" I shout. "Get out of here!"

Somehow the leaf blower gets even louder, and I start awake, jackknifing in my bed. Blearily I look around to find there's no bar, no Ben, and a heartbreaking lack of super-dirty foreplay. You know what I *do* hear? A goddamn lawnmower right outside my window. Checking the time on my phone, I growl. 8:45 on a Saturday morning. Someone's about to get it.

Getting out of bed, I dig through a box labeled "closet" and try to find my robe and some shoes. All I can find is an oversized hoodie and the Tweety Bird slippers Asher gave me for Christmas. Whatever. I can be a badass even in cartoon slippers. My new next-door neighbor is an asshole and I don't care if I've never met them before, they're going to get a piece of my mind.

Making my way through the maze of boxes to the front door, I practice my speech. I'm almost positive we have county-mandated quiet hours that my douche canoe of a neighbor is violating. I nearly trip over Frankie, my tortoise, in the front entryway. I seriously don't know how she keeps getting out of her cage. I really need to set up some kind of escape-proof box for her this week.

Scooping up Frankie, I carry her outside with me, holding her close to keep the chill off her. March seems to be crawling by, colder and wetter than most years. Dew soaks my slippers the second I step onto my lawn. Dual Tweety Bird heads flop wetly as I stomp across my yard. I try to ignore the fact that my yard could use a little love, but my overgrown oak tree has strewn sticks everywhere that I have to avoid.

The Valley Oak really is a monster of a tree, lording over the entire front of my property. The previous owners planted a little garden in front of the porch with lots of succulents and drought-resistant greenery. They reassured me over and over that the tough little plants need little attention, but I'm terrible at gardening. I've killed every plant I've ever been responsible for. Little purple flowers are blooming on a row of bushes and I silently apologize to them, both for the fate which they cannot escape and for the ass-chewing they are about to witness.

I eye the guy mowing. Even with his back to me, he's an impressive sight. He's wearing a torso-hugging Henley, muscles flexing everywhere I look and, god help me, I can't stop looking. His body looks like someone carved it out of marble and breathed life into it. He's huge. Crazy tall and just... thick all over. He turns the mower back towards me and I'm pretty sure my mouth is hanging open as I watch him get closer.

It's Ben.

Ben from the bar.

The same Ben who was just starring in my super-dirty dream like four minutes ago.

Oh no. Jesus, god in heaven.

I should just turn around and run back inside before he sees me in all of my rumpled, soggy, Tweety-Bird-slippered glory. I just have to stop watching him, which is a lot harder than it sounds. Maybe I can duck behind those bushes?!

Too late.

Ben looks up, and we make eye contact. The engine on the mower cuts out and the sudden silence is deafening. There's a rogue blade of grass on his cheek. He brushes it away and straightens his glasses. And oh god, I *really* like those glasses. His curly hair is rumpled, falling in his face as he

15

scrunches his eyebrows in confusion. He looks around like he's trying to figure out where I came from.

"Lilah? What are you doing here?" Even as he asks, his mouth pulls up at one side in a crooked grin.

"I just moved in yesterday," I blurt out as Ben steps close enough that I can see the shots of gold that run through his brown eyes. Holy mother of god. He was handsome in the dim atmosphere of the bar, but in broad daylight? This man is a god. And his voice! I wish I could just roll around in that Southern accent. People shouldn't be this pretty outside of magazines. I have to make a conscious effort not to melt into a puddle of goo at his feet.

Ben cocks his eyebrow at Frankie, who is making the world's slowest bid for freedom and snapping his jaw in Ben's direction.

"Nice attack turtle," Ben says with a smile.

"She's a tortoise, not a turtle," I say, defending my pet.

"Cute," Ben says. I think he's still talking about Frankie, but he's looking straight into my eyes and there's something hungry about his gaze. I'm suddenly aware of how close he's standing. When did he get so close? And why does he have to smell so good? He is... intoxicating. I just want to lean in and sniff him.

"I haven't seen a tortoise in years. What's her name?" Ben says as he reaches out to touch Frankie's shell, brushing his fingers over mine.

"Frankie," I murmur. His hands are so big they make mine look almost childlike. It makes me wonder what those big warm hands would feel like on other parts of my body. I really wouldn't mind snuggling into his chest. He looks like he gives amazing hugs. Hugs could be platonic, right? I guess it wouldn't be platonic if he had his shirt off. And it definitely wouldn't be platonic for very long if he ran those hands up and down my body...

Ben is looking at me like he's waiting for a response and I realize that I've been standing here like an idiot staring at his chest, thinking dirty, sexy things about him for way too long. He is so, so far out of my league.

"Sorry, I spaced. What did you say?" I shake my head and pray I'm not

16

blushing.

"Since you're already up, how about that brunch?" Ben repeats himself with a winning smile.

"I... I..."

I what?! I want to have brunch? I want to have your babies? I want to climb you like the majestic man-tree you are? If my lady taco was in charge she'd be screaming *"Yes, Yes, YES!"* right about now. Why can't I just drag him inside and have my way with him?

"I can't. I have to unpack," I say lamely as my vagina cries out in misery. I swear he has some kind of voodoo magic over my hormones, which is all the more reason for me to get away from him.

His face falls a little, betraying his disappointment for a split second before blinding me with the full force of his devastatingly dimpled grin. "Maybe another time. Let me know if you need anything. I work from home, so I'm usually around."

I'd be lying if I said I didn't watch his ass walk back to the mower. I'm in trouble. So, so much trouble.

***

A few hours later, I'm still feeling tired and grumpy from my rude awakening. I walk into the bakery and hear my sister Olive squeal with excitement. The sound alarms me, but the giant hug she gives me is so full of joy that I can't help but smile.

"Lilah, you'll never guess," Olive says, practically bouncing off the ceiling with excitement.

"You're probably right about that," I reply. "Also is there coffee? My sleep-in was disturbed by this total asshole--"

"Did you tell her yet?" calls a male voice from behind the counter. I look behind the glass countertop, surprised to see my soon-to-be brother-in-law

17

Brooks placing a cookie on a small delicate plate. Brooks is a contractor, and he doesn't usually work behind the counter at Olive's bakery. He looks ridiculous in the little blue apron, but the grin he's giving Olive makes it clear he doesn't care. He'd probably wear a tutu if he thought it would make her happy.

"Not yet," Olive says with a smile.

"Ok, what is it? You're both driving me nuts. Also give me a cookie."

Brooks hands me a cookie and I take a big bite as Olive steers me to a small table by the window. "So, I've been doing the math, and things are going really well, especially with the classes, and I think I can finally afford to hire you full time!"

I blink at her. "Wait, are you serious?"

"Dead serious!" Olive crows. "Isn't that exciting? No more Terry for you. No more artisan pickles. Only artisan cookies and cakes from now on!"

"Olive, are you sure? I don't want you to stretch yourself too thin--"

"I'm sure. I wouldn't do it unless I thought it would be better for both you and me. You're too smart. You'd figure it out."

I take another bite of my cookie and shake my head.

"Are you happy?" Olive asks, suddenly concerned. "If you'd rather not be here, that's ok too, I don't want to force you--"

"Are you kidding? I'm delirious! I'm just in shock."

Olive squeals again and jumps up to get me a coffee. I sit back in my chair and sigh, feeling a weight lift from my shoulders. Now all I have to do is give Terry my notice. I can't fucking wait.

Chapter 5: Ben

I'm in the zone, going through every file on the Senator's computer one by one, looking for the proof I need. This might be the easiest hacking job I've ever picked up. His passwords are all the same: his first name followed by 69. Even his security pin is 6969. I mean, come on. I could have used a challenge.

I only need half my brain for this job. The other half is wondering where Lilah's been. I haven't caught so much as a glimpse of her since the mowing incident. She didn't even come out to yell at me when I cut my grass this morning. So disappointing.

I find the file I'm looking for, make copies, and send it to the major news outlets and police from his own email address. I put a base-level encryption on the file so he can't delete anything without the help of someone who has at least double his IQ. It's a low bar.

I'm backing out of the system when I'm startled by the beeping of my security alarm. Somebody or something tripped the sensor by my front door. Judging by the time, it's probably just a fox or the raccoons again, but I quickly pull up my app and check the video feed. Lilah is on my porch.

Why is Lilah pacing my porch? Better question, why is Lilah pacing my porch at 2:45 in the morning? I try to turn the volume up, but the cameras have terrible audio quality. I make a mental note to replace them as I watch her.

The way she's pacing suggests she's not in trouble... but unless I'm mistaken, she's drunk. The little stumble and sway are a dead giveaway. I hurry to the door in my pajama pants. I don't like the thought of her being outside, alone, in the middle of the night. Does she have any sense of self-preservation at all?

When I open the door, Lilah has her back to me and she's walking away. She either doesn't notice or doesn't hear the door open as she takes another step and mutters, "... stupid. So, so stupid."

"Lilah? Are you ok?" I ask quietly, trying not to startle her. She lets out a terrified scream before wheeling around to face me and clamping her hands over her mouth. Mr. Miller's dog barks his head off three houses down.

"Sorry," she whispers guiltily, her eyes wide.

She's wearing a short red dress, all hips and curves and long stretches of leg. She's so beautiful and looks so soft and touchable. I've never wanted a woman like I want her. It's like a physical ache to be this close and not touch her. I'd do almost anything to touch her, taste her, and feel her writhe underneath me.

Great. And now I have half a chub just thinking about it. I'd feel guilty, but she looks me up and down, taking her time as she licks her lips. I nearly groan out loud. How can such a tiny gesture be so fucking sexy?

"Sorry," she repeats as she shakes her head a little, seeming to get a hold of herself. "It's so late. I didn't mean to wake you up."

There's a slight slur to her words and even in this light I can tell her makeup is a little smudged. She's definitely drunk and it's so damn adorable, but now I'm going to spend every night worried out of my damn mind about whether or not she's getting home safe.

"I was up... but are you ok? You seem a little drunk." I grin at her as I lean against the door frame, crossing my legs and hiding Mr. Happy before he makes an unwelcome debut.

"I'm not drunk! You're drunk!" she says indignantly before hiccupping. "Ok, I'm a little tipsy. But I'm *not* drunk!" The black lace bra peeking out of her dress and the mussed makeup are telling another story. I'm torn between wanting to see more of that bra and worrying about her. Something about her sets off every protective instinct I have... but I'm still me, and I can't help pushing her buttons.

"Why are you drunk—excuse me, tipsy—and pacing my porch at 3 am?" I ask her with a chuckle.

"My sister got engaged, and we were celebrating downtown."

I nod at her like this explains everything.

20

"And Sven dropped me off at home." She hiccups and examines her shoe, covered in grass clippings, scowling at the green flecks. It's hard not to smile at her lips pursing like--

Hold up. Who the fuck is Sven?! And why is this douche dropping her off but not making sure she gets inside? Especially when she's dressed like this? I hate him already.

"Why do you look mad?" She squints at me and sways a little.

"I'm not mad. It just seems like your date should have made sure you were safe inside before driving off." Do I sound sour? Absolutely. I do.

Lilah cackles, hunching over and wrapping her arms around her stomach as she laughs like I'm the funniest guy in the world. She's giving me an amazing view down her dress, but I turn my eyes skyward, cursing my mother for raising me to be a decent guy. I only peek once, because it's a damn fine view.

"You're jealous of *Sven*?" she wheezes.

"I'm not jealous, he just sounds like a douche," I retort.

"He's my friend's 50-year-old driver. And he's gay. I'm not dating him."

That's a relief. She's still giggling, little hiccups mixed in as she wipes a tear from her eye.

"Well, as happy as I am to give you a good laugh, why are you out here in the middle of the night?" I ask.

Lilah pulls her back straight and sets her shoulders, a stern tilt in her eyebrows. "I came off to you!" She jumbles up her words and does an adorable pause as she looks up at her eyebrows. My eyes go wide and all the blood in my body rushes south as I imagine her getting herself off. "I came to tell you off." She sighs as if she's frustrated, and squeezes her eyes shut. "I'm-not-that-drunk-you-just-make-me-nervous," she whispers in a single breath.

Then she opens her eyes and glares at me. I'm sure she thinks she looks fierce, but everything she does is so damn cute that I can't help smiling.

"What am I getting told off for this time?" I ask. "And why do I make you nervous?"

"Stop grinning at me like that! Put the dimples away!" Her scowl slips a little as she hiccups again. "The Saturday morning mowing has to stop. I swear to Jesus, if you wake me up with that thing one more time, I'll put sugar in its gas tank."

"Threatening my lawnmower?" I tsk as I step down onto the porch. "Not very neighborly of you, Pickles."

Lilah closes the distance between us and pokes me in the chest, craning her neck back to look up at me. "Listen here, you big beefcake, you've woken me up two Saturdays in a row! Where do you get off?!"

"In bed, usually. I'm not averse to the shower, though. How about you?" I choose to take the beef cake thing as a compliment. I'd be her beefcake anytime she wants. I shouldn't push her buttons, but the color rising in her cheeks as I rile her up is sexy as hell. She's a spitfire and I have to admit, I love it.

Lilah's face blushes all the way up into her hairline and she sputters, "Wha- No! That's not what I meant! I--"

"Relax, princess," I say, holding my hands out to calm her down. "I promise I'll let you sleep this one off tomorrow morning." Lilah takes a deep breath, and she's standing so close that her breasts brush against my bare chest. Her breath hitches as she stares into my eyes, body frozen for a couple seconds before smacking me on the arm and letting out a sound halfway between a growl and a scream of frustration.

She turns on her heel and marches across my yard toward her own. I watch her until she makes it back to her house. "Don't forget to lock your door!" I call out. She doesn't look back, but she does flip me off as she opens the front door. I stand still on my porch as I strain to hear the clunk of the deadbolt in the quiet night. If I don't hear it, I'll go do it myself.

A loud but satisfying clunk echoes on the quiet street. I can only imagine how hard she had to turn it to make that much noise. I watch for a minute to make sure she stays inside, then head back to bed.

22

Chapter 6: Lilah

Oh fu-huh-huuuuck, I think as I roll over in bed. My head is *killing* me. Cracking one eye open, I can see the sun pouring through the window and it is straight torture. I definitely should have pumped the brakes on the mojitos last night.

I groan as I sit up and look around. My dress from last night is draped over the lamp. I must have thrown my bra at the laundry hamper and missed, but at least I found an oversized t-shirt to sleep in.

My heels are in the middle of the floor and... why are they all covered in grass clippings?! What the hell? I freeze as my brain starts to reboot. A memory flashes: a beefcake standing on a porch in his pajamas, grinning down at me. The smell of fresh cut grass in the air.

Oh no.

I pull my pillow over my face and scream into it as every embarrassing moment of last night floods back to me. I can't believe I woke Ben up in the middle of the night to yell at him. Oh god. I think I called him a beefcake. Like, out loud. What is wrong with me? And I definitely remember threatening to sugar his mower's gas tank. I'm not taking that one back, though. I'll even use the expensive sugar we use for crème brûlée at the bakery. That's what he deserves for calling me 'Princess.' What a dick.

The worst part is that I'm not sure I just wanted to yell at him. If that conversation had gone differently, I think I gladly would have hopped into bed with him.

After Brooks broke up girl's night and kidnapped my sister for things I *do not* want to think about, we bounced from bar to bar. Men hit on Julia all night and she pretended they didn't exist, sending back drink after drink. Chelsea and Matt were all over each other and watching them together made me lonely. After their chauffeur, Sven, dropped me off at home, I stood inside my front door and fought a war with my hormones.

Telling myself I was just going to nicely ask him to stop mowing made it seem okay to go knock on his door, at least in Tipsyland. But as soon as I got there, I knew it was a terrible idea. I couldn't lie to myself convincingly enough to ignore the fact that I've been spending a lot of time fantasizing about Ben. I don't remember knocking but when he opened the door, shirtless, my (not so) carefully laid plans flew out the window.

I scream into my pillow again, equal parts embarrassment and sexual frustration.

Rolling over to look at my phone, I'm surprised to see it's 11:15 am. At least Ben kept his promise to let me sleep in. I'm supposed to be at the bakery at noon to help Olive with this afternoon's class, and I have just enough time to shower and clean up my mess from last night.

After a shower, some coffee and a coat of mascara, no one should be able to tell I'm hungover, but it only takes Olive one glance at my face to figure me out. As soon as I roll into the bakery, she's giving me the side eye. She tries to suppress a smirk as she asks, "How was the rest of last night?"

I groan in response. "Sally got us all good and drunk and then ordered another round of tequila shots. I'm dying. If I run to the dumpster, don't mind me; it's just that I like privacy when I puke."

She pats me sympathetically. "Did you put your notice in?" She's trying not to sound too eager, but I know she's excited for me to quit the bar.

"Yup, I sure as hell can't keep working with Terrance. One more week and I'll be free of the most hostile workplace in Sonoma."

"Yeah, no kidding. Speaking of which, how did the slime lord take it when you put in your notice?"

I laugh humorlessly. "About as well as could be expected of that piece of shit."

Olive reaches over and squeezes my hand. "I'm so glad you won't be working there anymore. You can finally be here full time!"

"Well, I had a thought about that..." I hedge.

Olive sucks in a breath as if she's nervous, but she doesn't say anything. Instead she waits for me to continue.

24

"I want to expand the coffee roasting."

"Yeah?" Olive's eyebrow stays aloft, but her look shifts from worried to intrigued. "What are you thinking?"

"We only use the roaster for about an hour a day as it is. We could hire someone on part-time and roast coffee for local restaurants and markets. I think even a few hours a day would be enough to keep every shop in town supplied. I'm good at marketing and sales and I can finally put a little of my education to use."

Olive gives me an impressed smile. "Hell yes. Go for it."

"Really? That's it?" I ask her.

"Yes, really. It's a great idea. I don't have the time or inclination to do it, but if you do, I'm all in!"

"Well, that was easy," I mutter.

"Were you afraid I'd say no?" She shakes her head. "Lilah, this bakery is just as much yours as mine. At least in spirit." Olive grins at me, and I feel lighter than I have in weeks.

"Quitting the bar means I need to use the trust fund to pay my mortgage." I say, looking at my hands.

"Good!" Olive gives me an exasperated look and backhands my shoulder. "You should have been using it all along! Grandpa left them to us for a reason. He wanted you to have a better life than pouring tourists drinks and getting hit on by your slimy boss and half the assholes that come through town."

"I know. I bet Grandpa would have punched Terry for me."

"Yeah, that and he would have bought the bar and destroyed Terry publicly as a parting shot." Olive laughs as Brooks, her fiancé, strides into the kitchen looking for her. Her entire face lights up when she sees him.

"Ready for lunch?" he asks, pulling her toward him. I pointedly look down at the almond flour I'm scaling out for the Macaron Madness class. Olive and Brooks are disgustingly cute together. I'm happy for them, obviously. I mean, I did kind of nudge them together when they both had their heads up their respective asses. But sure, maybe I'm a little jealous. They're clearly made for each other, and I can't help but wonder what it would feel like to find someone like that.

My own experiences with dating have been so catastrophic that I don't know if I can make myself try ever again.

Luis, the head baker, interrupts my pouty thoughts with a very tactful, "Who hit you with the hangover stick?"

"Ha-ha. I would be fine if Brooks hadn't kidnapped Olive from girl's night. She's the voice of reason and the one who switches out my drinks for water when I get too tipsy. All my drunk actions and subsequent hangover are Brooks' fault." I scowl at my future brother-in-law, but he just laughs.

"Yeah, but she *really* likes it when I kidnap her."

"Ew," Luis and I say in unison.

Olive laughs and smacks Brooks on the chest. "Give me a second. I'll meet you up front."

He kisses her adoringly and walks back out the way he came.

"You could have switched out your own drinks last night. That's what I always do when I go drinking with Sally. If I didn't swap out some of my martinis for water in a martini glass, I'd never make it through a single night. I swear, that woman has the alcohol tolerance of a rhino," Olive says as she wraps the sheet tray of chocolate chip cupcakes.

"And take responsibility for my own actions? Hard pass," I joke. "Besides, how would I embarrass myself in front of my hot-as-fuck neighbor? It's not like you can wake someone up in the middle of the night to yell at them sober."

Olive's hands freeze mid-task as she turns to look at me with enormous eyes.

"Noooo. What did you do?"

"Matt and Chelsea asked Sven to drop me off last night. I was all worked up because Ben woke me up two weekends in a row with the stupid mowing. I mean, who even mows their lawn every week? Anyway, I was all salty about it and I drunkenly decided I should tell him to knock it off."

Olive leans her elbows on the counter and covers her face with both hands, groaning at my poor decision making. Yeah, she knows where this is going.

"It seemed like a good idea at the time," I try to defend myself. "So anyway, I woke Ben up at 3 am. Or maybe he was already awake? He said he wasn't sleeping, and I doubt he'd lie to make me feel better. I tried to tell him off, but he just thought I was being funny. He wouldn't stop grinning at me. I think I yelled at him to put his dimples away. I definitely called him a beefcake and poked him in the chest."

Olive is laughing so hard she's wheezing as she asks, "Holy shit, dude. What did he say after you assaulted him?"

Just recalling it makes me scowl. "He called me Princess and said he'd let me sleep in today."

Olive cackles. "He called you 'Princess' and you let him live? If one of our brothers had called you something like that, you would have destroyed him."

"Yeah, well, I took the high road and left instead," I say, holding my head high and trying to preserve the last shred of dignity I have left.

"You say 'took the high road' but I know you and I've seen you drunk. You mean you shrieked at him and stormed off."

"I hate you sometimes, you know that?" I tell her.

She hugs me aggressively, pinning my arms to my sides and kisses me on the temple. "You love me all the time. You just hate that I know you so well." She squeezes me even harder when I grumble at her. "Say it! Say you love me!" she demands.

"Fine, fine! I love you!" I huff. Olive laughs and lets me go. Luis shakes his head at us from the back where he's taking inventory. "Go eat with Brooks," I tell Olive, shooing her out of the kitchen and taking the tray of cupcakes from her. She blows me a kiss as she heads out front.

Luis is muttering in Spanish, something about "chicas locas."

"I heard that!" I tell him.

"You're just like your sister," he says, rolling his eyes at me.

Chapter 7: Lilah

My last night at Blue Ruin flies by. It's after 2 am before we finish closing, but my coworkers throw me a mini party in the back. They present me with cupcakes and a teddy bear with a martini glass. It's not like I'm moving away, but I appreciate the gesture. Mostly I'm just glad Terry wasn't working tonight.

It's pouring rain when we walk out, so we hide under the awning, hugging goodbyes before running to our cars. The spring rain is icy cold, little bits of hail bouncing off the pavement. I'm soaked by the time I get to my Jeep and already shivering when I wrench the door open.

Tossing Martini the Bear in the passenger seat, I climb in and turn the key, eager to turn up the heat. Nothing. I try it a second time, because maybe I'm an idiot and I forgot how to turn a car on? Mother. Fucking. Nothing. The damn thing doesn't even turn over. Picking up my phone, I plan to use it as a flashlight to look under the hood until I see that it's at a whopping 4%. I snort at myself because even if I had all the battery power in the world, I would still have no idea what to do with anything under the hood of my car. This is what mechanic brothers are for.

I rack my brain, trying to decide who to call. It's almost 3 am, so my gran and brothers and sisters will all be asleep. Maybe one of my coworkers? But they've all booked it out of Sonoma by now...

Luis! He's the only person who I know for a fact will be awake. No doubt he's elbow deep in baguette dough right now, but the bakery is only five minutes away. He could rescue me and be back at the bakery in less than 15 minutes and I can just crash in Olive's old apartment above the bakery.

I lock the car doors, just to be safe, and call Luis. He doesn't answer the first time and my phone is down to 3%. I can't help thinking about the four charged battery packs I have sitting in a drawer at home. They're so helpful now, aren't they? I try Luis again and thankfully he answers on the second ring.

"What's up, homeslice?" he asks. I can hear music blasting in the background, and I guarantee he was singing at the top of his lungs until I called.

"Hey, my Jeep won't start. I'm stranded outside Blue Ruin and my phone battery is about to die. Can you pick me up?" Rain is pounding on the roof and windows of my car, so loud I have to cover my other ear just to hear him.

Luis sighs, but I hear him turn off the music. "I'll be right there. Stay in your car and lock the doors."

"Worry wart," I tease him.

"Lilah, if anything happens to you before I can pick you up, your Gran would skin me alive."

Laughing, I promise to keep the doors locked and thank him before hanging up the phone. Leaning my head back, I close my eyes, willing myself to relax while I wait for Luis.

Gran would never skin her next-door neighbor alive. After our dad abandoned us with Gran, Luis became almost like an adoptive father to us. He even took Julia to her Father-Daughter dance in fifth grade. His two boys, Mateo and Javier, were like extra brothers that came and went as they pleased. They still do, come to think of it.

With all of us kids out of her house and Luis' two sons out of the state, Luis and Gran have become closer than ever. And by close, I mean they've been pranking each other on the reg, and getting drunk together on Saturday nights. I'd appreciate it more if they didn't target me for their prank calls.

Looking out the window at the sign for Blue Ruin, it's weird to think this was my last night at the bar. I'm happy enough to leave it behind, but I've been doing it for so long that I feel a little... un-anchored. Which is silly because I have so much work between the bakery and getting the coffee going.

A couple minutes later, I see Luis' headlights as he turns into the parking lot and parks alongside me. Not a moment too soon; I'm freezing and dying to get warm. I grab my stuff and hop into his car.

"You're a lifesaver!" I tell him before I'm blinded by another car pulling

30

into the parking lot with its high beams on. Jackass. The driver uses the lot to turn around and go back the way they came, and I resist the urge to flip them off for scorching my retinas.

"Anytime," Luis says, patting me on the arm. "Jesus, you're freezing!" He turns up the heat before turning all the vents in my direction.

"Thanks," I say with a shiver. "I'll just crash at Olive's tonight," I tell Luis. He chuckles and shakes his head.

"Nah, I'll drop you off at your place. I'm ahead this morning and I've got 45 minutes left on the rise for the baguettes, anyway. You called at the exact right time."

"How are the boys?" I ask as I hold my icy fingers in front of the blasting hot air.

Luis chuckles. "Oh, you know them. Mateo is getting into trouble every time he gets shore leave, and I don't think Javier ever stops working."

We're outside my bungalow five minutes later and Luis watches to make sure I get inside ok. After admitting to making inebriated threats to Ben's mower, I suspect no one will ever drop me off and leave without making sure I'm inside again.

My phone vibrates in my pocket and for a second I'm worried Luis got in an accident or someone's been hurt, but when I look at the screen it just says, "Unknown Number." I growl and silence it. There is a special place in hell for telemarketers that can't even keep it to business hours.

I peek out the window at Ben's house. He's been so quiet the last couple days. Not a power tool or weed whacker to be heard. It has been glorious, even if I am slightly disappointed to lose the eye candy. Maybe he took my threats seriously? I laugh at myself as I change into my pajamas and toss Martini the Bear on the bed. I doubt that man takes anything seriously. Least of all me.

Chapter 8: Ben

A sliver of sunlight is glinting off my alarm clock, blinding me. I was already awake when the sun came up. Awake, with a serious case of morning wood. Fantasizing about Lilah isn't cutting it lately. I'm a walking ball of sexual frustration at this point. It's been a week since she drunkenly threatened me in that little red dress, and I've been slowly dying every day since. If I could just see Lilah, I'd be happy. Bonus points if I can talk to her. I have a plan, but it's not a good one.

Desperation finally overrules my common sense and just a few minutes later I'm dressed and walking toward the shed in my backyard. An angel and a demon are having a cage match on my shoulder. The demon is winning. I unlock the shed door and pull it open. Inside, my shiny black lawnmower glints in the sunshine that filters through the shed windows.

I know I shouldn't do this, but she's been avoiding me since her drunk visit and I just know she's embarrassed. I can't get her out of my head. It plays on repeat; the red dress, the way she laughed and then turned around and threatened my lawnmower... Even in heels, she barely came up to my shoulders, but it didn't stop her from poking me in the chest ferociously. I guess I've gotten used to the way most people look at me. I hit my growth spurt in middle school and didn't stop growing until I outstripped everyone I knew. It's not just my height either. I bulked out like a linebacker the second I started lifting weights. Most people find me alarmingly large, but Lilah doesn't seem to mind at all. She just looked up at me with those stunning green eyes, trying to glare at me. Fearless.

Maybe that's why I'm completely distracted by her. In the end, the "why" of it doesn't really matter. I just know that my need to see her again is almost all-consuming. And maybe this is a dick move, but I think it's my best option at this point. Am I being a petulant child? Maybe. Is it worth it if I get to see her again? Absolutely. Especially if she comes out wearing those little bird slippers again.

As I wheel my lawnmower out of the shed, I wonder how mad she'll be.

Chapter 9: Lilah

The roar of the lawnmower outside my window rips me out of another *wonderfully* filthy dream.

"NO! No-no-no-no-no! Why?!" I yell as I fling the covers off.

I'm going to kill him. I am going to kill Ben Clark with my bare hands. I can see it now: his stupidly handsome face realizing that he just fucked with the wrong girl. In my revenge fantasy, I elegantly spring from my bed, ready to take on my jackass neighbor. But reality sucks and my feet tangle in the top sheet and I fall out of bed with all the grace of a drunk panda, smacking my face on the end table as I go down.

"Ow! Ow-fucking-ow!"

That's just great. Add a head injury on top of the exhaustion. It's bad enough that my Jeep wouldn't start after work last night. Nothing is quite as fun as discovering a dead battery at 3 am. Now I get to deal with this jackass, a throbbing headache, and finding someone to jumpstart my car all before I even start my workday. Awesome.

I get to my feet, a little wobbly but mostly okay. I even manage to make it to my front door without hurting myself again. Propelled mostly by rage, I stomp across my own overgrown lawn, hugging myself. It's warmed up a bit now that the sun is out, but I still should have grabbed a robe or at least put on a bra.

"Why is he like this?" I mutter to myself before yelling, "You asshole! You said you wouldn't do this again!"

The big ape can't hear me. His mower is running at a million decibels, and his big, stupid, muscled back is turned. I studiously ignore the way those back muscles ripple as he pushes his evil machine through the grass. That sweat dripping down his thick arms? Not distracting at all. I won't even acknowledge how those low-slung athletic shorts cling to his glorious ass and thighs. Nope. None of it.

I make it to the edge of my property and huff, standing barefoot with my hands on my hips. Ben is just turning his mower back when he sees me. His eyes widen and he kills the engine just as I yell his name at the top of my lungs again.

His face brightens and his mouth pulls up at one corner in the beginnings of a smirk. He's sporting a short beard along his jaw, well, something between a 5 o'clock shadow and a beard. Whatever you call it, it's sexy as hell. He has a white t-shirt tossed over one shoulder and he straightens his black-framed glasses as he walks towards me. I die a little. Why does he have to look so good and be so damn annoying?

"Hey Lilah. What can I..." he trails off as he looks at my face and his dimples disappear. "Jesus, what happened there?" Ben reaches out to touch my forehead and I ignore the little thrill that runs up my spine.

"YOU happened!" I snap back. "You and that stupid lawn- Ow!" His fingers graze the bump where my head connected with my end table and they come away with blood. I've been running on anger and adrenaline since I was so rudely awoken, but the sight of the blood on his fingers—my blood—and the concern on Ben's face is enough to tamp down my rage. My hand flies up to my head and I touch the enormous lump with dawning horror.

"Lilah, are you ok? Do you have a first aid kit?" Ben asks me gently. His eyebrows are drawn together in worry, and his ever-present cocky smirk is replaced with concern.

"I think I have some Bandaids," I reply shakily. I honestly couldn't be sure if I even have those, but even if I do, there's no way in hell I'm letting Ben into my house right now. I know for a fact that I have at least six bras and a dozen panties hanging on a drying rack in my living room. Note to self: buy a house with a decent laundry room next time.

"How do you not have a first aid kit?" Ben asks me, his voice teasing.

"I just moved in, jackass," I reply sarcastically. He's still smiling at me like it's adorable that I swore at him.

"Well, come on," he says as he takes my elbow and starts leading me toward his house. The independent part of me, which is like 99%, wants to pull my arm free and scold him for leading me like a child. The other 1% is

34

loving the way his hand feels on me. He's huge and so is his hand, a little calloused, and so warm on my skin. He's not being overly rough with me, but he's not treating me like a delicate little flower either. I can't say that I hate it. I bet he's amazing in bed. A delicious little shiver runs through me at the runaway thought, and Ben gives me a concerned look.

"Are you cold?" he asks.

"No. I'm fine."

Although I'm seriously questioning my sanity right now. If true crime podcasts have taught me anything, you never hitchhike, and you never go into some guy's house when you barely know him. I can see nosy old Mr. Miller watching us while he waters his flower beds, so at least there will be a witness if I disappear.

"Um, you're not a serial killer, right? Like, you're not going to tie me up in your basement or anything?"

Ben raises an eyebrow. "Not without your consent," he replies.

I bark out a decidedly unladylike laugh.

Joke or not, the thought of him tying me to his bed and fucking me senseless has a certain appeal. Not that I'd ever admit that out loud.

"Consent not given," I tell him as he opens the front door for me.

Ben quirks an eyebrow up at me. "Fair enough. Bondage not your thing?" he asks. I can feel my face flush. I'm suddenly very aware that he's still touching my arm.

"I wouldn't know. And who says things like that?" I give him a defiant look even though I know my face is beet red.

Ben grins down at me as he leads me to his couch. "Sorry, I didn't mean to make you blush. Here, sit down." He holds up a hand. "Stay."

I roll my eyes and glare at him as he chuckles and walks down the hallway toward the master bedroom. His house is the mirror image of mine; a one-story bungalow with narrow hallways, small bedrooms, and not nearly enough natural light. Through the gap in the doorway I can see a large four poster bed with rumpled covers and pillows tossed all over the place. I have to forcefully push the mental image of him sprawled across that bed out of my head.

Instead, I focus on the living room, anything to avoid looking at his bed again. Photographs cover the walls of his house. Some look like his family, combinations of Ben with his mom, dad, and a sister. But most of the photos are landscapes and nature shots. Deserts, enormous agave, mountains, and Aspen trees. They're beautiful and I wonder where he bought them.

I'm distracted when Ben reemerges with a huge first aid bag. And maybe it's the wrong moment to notice, but even the way he walks is a turn on. His stride is masculine and purposeful. Kind of like everything else about him. I feel like a tiny clumsy hobbit next to him.

Ben sets the bag on the coffee table before pulling the entire thing closer. When he sits next to me, the couch dips and I slide towards him. His thigh presses against mine and he's alarmingly close. Maybe I should scoot away? Yes, I definitely should. But I really don't want to.

So… I let him crowd me and I pretend like I don't notice that he didn't put a shirt on when he disappeared to get the bag. His tan skin is still glistening and bare. Sitting this close I can see the dusting of light brown hair on his chest and the sheen of sweat that *really* shouldn't be sexy, but he's got this Henry Cavill thing going on and all I can think of is Clark Kent running shirtless in the rain.

Aaaand I'm staring. My eyes shoot up when I realize what I'm doing, and I must have a guilty look on my face because Ben looks smug as hell. Did I just softly sigh while inappropriately fantasizing about a man sitting right next to me? I must have hit my head harder than I thought, because I am clearly concussed.

"Shit. Sorry," I mutter.

"Why?" Ben laughs. "Look all you want. I don't mind." He's still chuckling as he pulls little packets, gauze, and tape out of his bag. He puts on a pair of gloves and opens an antibacterial cleansing cloth. "Look, this might sting but you need to hold still." I nod as he leans in even closer and touches it to my forehead. He's not wrong, it does sting a bit as he gently

36

wipes my forehead clean of blood, but I don't care. His face is inches from mine and sweet baby Jesus, I can smell him. He smells like fresh soap and sweat and when he breathes, his breath is vaguely minty. Meanwhile, I rolled out of bed, literally, and stomped over here unbrushed, unshowered, and only half dressed. Nice.

Ben pulls his head back a bit to look at my face as he works on me.

"Are you ok? Does that hurt?" he asks.

"Oh, no. I mean, yes a little but it doesn't bother me," I reply. "I mean, I have a high pain tolerance. I'm not going to be a baby about a little antiseptic." He smiles at me as I babble. His eyes have that calculating intensity again, but they never lose the sweet-looking crinkles at the corners. I snap my mouth shut and resist the urge to fix my hair. I don't think I even want to know how bad it is.

Ben squeezes antibiotic ointment onto a Q-Tip and then his big hand is cupping my jaw, holding me still while he spreads the ointment on my forehead. I watch his eyes as he focuses on his work. This feels weirdly intimate and I hate to admit that I'm disappointed when he lets my face go, but I hold still as he tapes a piece of gauze to my face.

"There. No more gaping head wound." He sits back with a smile and cracks a disposable ice pack, holding it to my forehead. "Hold that there for 15 minutes." He collects the trash from fixing me up and as he stands, he says, "Tell me again how all of this was my fault?"

I suddenly remember my anger and follow him into the kitchen, ice pressed against my face and my free hand on my hip.

"Tell me the honest truth: are you mowing this early just to fuck with me?" I ask.

He crosses his arms across his chest and leans back against the kitchen counter as he tosses the wrappers in the trash can. He looks down, trying to hide a grin, and his sandy brown curls fall over his forehead.

"Yes."

I'm seeing red. I don't care how fucking hot he is or how good he smells.

I don't even care that I like the way he touches me. I hate his smug ass.

Chapter 10: Ben

Honesty is the best policy, right? Usually I'd say so, but Lilah is glaring at me like I kicked a puppy. Color rises in her cheeks and her wide green eyes flash with anger.

"Why?!" Her pretty mouth hangs open as she searches my face for a reasonable explanation. She propels herself away from the counter she was leaning on and pokes me in the chest, and despite her anger, she's rather gentle with the poking. She smells like cinnamon and fresh laundry.

"Are you trying to get back at me for something?" she sputters.

I grab her wrist to stop her from poking me again, or maybe it's just because I want to touch her. I let my thumb skim along the side of her hand, feeling her smooth softness. I bet she's like that all over. She scowls at me with renewed anger. The morning light is pouring through the window, illuminating her like a tiny, beautiful, fiercely angry angel.

"Calm down, Princess. I wasn't trying to be a dick."

"So, what? It's just a fun little game for you? Riling up the neighbors? Waking us up at all hours? Yeah, doesn't sound like a dick move at all."

"Jesus, you're one to talk," I say with a smile. I can feel her heartbeat in her wrist, the pulse growing stronger and faster with every sentence we exchange. "After turning up on my doorstep at 2 am just to yell at me?"

"That- that was different!"

"Why? Because you were drunk and wanted to see me?"

"I did NOT want to see you. I just wanted you to be a decent person, but *clearly* that was too much to ask."

There's a pull between us, like a rubber band drawing her closer every second until we're toe to toe. Our height differences force her to crane her neck up so she can glare at me. This close up, I can see the tiny freckle under her left eye and the flutter of her lashes as she blinks angrily at me. It's impossible not to smile at her. I've never smiled this much in my whole damn life, but my face hurts when I'm around her.

"You're fucking adorable when you're mad," I tell her.

"I am not!" she says indignantly.

"Yeah, you really are..."

She stares at me, eyes narrowed for two lengthy breaths. There is electricity between us, and I know I'm not the only one who's feeling it. Without warning, Lilah's arm shoots out, her warm little hand grabbing the back of my neck as she pulls me down. Her soft lips press against mine, kissing me fiercely. For a second, I'm so shocked I don't move. She takes my stillness the wrong way, pulling back and looking appalled at herself as she whispers. "Oh, my god. I'm so sor--"

I cut her off, cupping her face in my hands and kissing her back, swallowing the apology that I have zero interest in hearing. Her hands, pressed to my bare chest, are so warm. I want to feel all of her pressing against me, skin to skin. I'm not the only one who needs more because Lilah is leaning into me, her hips and stomach pressing against me. I sure as fuck can't stop my body from responding to the feel of her.

Running a hand through the soft hair at the back of her head, I wrap the other around her waist, pulling her closer, my hard-on pressing into her belly. Her lips part against mine and I feel the barest touch of her tongue against my lips, an invitation if there ever was one. I tighten my grip in her hair, taking control as my tongue slicks against hers.

Lilah moans, the sound muffled against my lips as she wraps her arms around my neck. She rocks her hips against me, teetering on her tiptoes. Jesus, she's so short. She's like a curvy little doll, and it makes me feel like a giant next to her. Gripping her ass, I straighten up and pop her on the kitchen counter, our lips never breaking contact.

The angle is even better like this, letting me claim her mouth as she wraps her bare thighs around my hips. I can feel the heat of her through my shorts and I'm aching to rip her clothes off and taste every fucking inch of her. The ways she moves against me, all soft skin and muffled pleasure, is intoxicating. I could lose myself in her forever.

40

Chapter 11: Lilah

Oh god. So good. Soooo good. Ben picks me up and sets me on the counter like I weigh nothing. His hips press between my thighs, demanding to be closer as he wrestles control of the kiss. His lips are insistent but not frantic. He's all passion and contained power and it is *really* working for me. He has one hand in my hair, cupping the back of my head. His fingertips send little tingles down my spine as our tongues tangle. The other wraps around my lower back, holding my body flush against his.

What am I doing?! I shouldn't be doing this. It's too much, but I can't help myself as I wrap my legs around his waist. His steely length rubs against me and I moan. He smells amazing, like fresh ocean air, and he feels... *right*. He's so big that I feel like he could toss me if he wanted to, but instead he holds me like a treasure he can't stop touching. It's dangerously sexy, and he's ticking every box, including the ones I didn't even realize I had.

I've never felt chemistry like this. Every nerve in my body lights up when Ben strokes my back with his thumb and when his grip on my hair tightens it sends tingles of pleasure skittering up my spine.

His phone and watch both start pinging and I'm jarred back to reality. He pulls back, breaking the kiss to silence the phone.

"Sorry," he says as he looks at me under hooded eyes. His lips are swollen from kissing me and I touch my own lips, wondering if they look the same. His watch doesn't respond to his attempts to silence it, so he undoes the clasp and chucks it into the living room with a muttered, "fuck it."

I laugh, but the distraction gave me enough time to come to my senses. I can't just jump into bed with my new neighbor. There's a reason I don't date, and when this inevitably goes bad, I'll literally have to sell my house and move to get away from him.

I have to get out of here before the last pieces of my self control slip away. Seriously, I need to get a grip on my sanity. This is why we have vibrators.

Pressing my hands to his chest, I unwrap my legs from his body, just trying to get enough room to think straight. "I should go," I say.

His brow furrows in confusion. "I'm sorry... Did I do something...?" he trails off and I can see that he's worried he pushed me too far.

"No. No, this was equally my fault." I tell him as I look away. I can't meet his eyes because I'm not sure I'll be able to resist him if I do. I need to get out of here. I can't let this happen again and I know if I'm near him I won't be able to control myself. I press him back a little and he steps back, taking my hand as he helps me off of his counter. Jesus, he's sexy. Every little touch, even just the way he holds my hand in his, sends butterflies careening around in my stomach. Big, aggressive, horny butterflies.

"Thanks for bandaging me up," I say before trying to pull free and head for the front door. He grips my hand for a second, forcing me to turn around.

"Lilah, let me take you out for dinner tonight."

I freeze up like the spaz I am, my mouth hanging open as I try to find the right thing to say.

"I... I can't." I don't add that I am incapable of trusting anyone outside of my family. That agreeing to date him would be like taking my heart out of my chest and handing it to him, unprotected. Stupid and risky. I don't tell him he terrifies me. Not because of his size or anything he's done, but because the way he makes me feel is addictive.

I don't look up to see his reaction, just turn and walk out the door.

I rush home, trying to get my body back under control, but my thoughts are racing, running away from me. I can't shake the feeling that I left a piece of myself in Ben's kitchen. I don't feel quite whole, like there's a tiny little chamber in my soul that's echoing and empty.

I shut my front door and lean back against it. It has been a fucking *morning* and my body just betrayed me. One look from Ben and it gave me up. Not that I really blame my body. My head was there too and even though that bitch is usually pretty smart, she was all in. Ben was all smiles and dimples, but his eyes burned into me. I'm tingling everywhere he touched me, like my skin has been marked by his.

42

And oh, god, I am so wet. I'm seriously tempted to march back over there and throw myself in his hands just so he can take the ache away. I bet he's magnificent with those hands.

I'm exhausted and even though I'd like to go back to bed, I don't know if I could even fall back asleep at this point. I'd just lay in bed and pine after Ben.

I need a cold shower, and then I'll go to the bakery and help Olive. I'll be a couple hours early, but I might as well do something productive with all this pent-up energy. I take a quick shower, towel dry my hair, throwing on jeans and my favorite soft black t-shirt. I grab a clean chef coat out of my closet and head towards the front door. I only get two steps outside before I realize that my Jeep is still at Blue Ruin. That's just perfect.

Tapping out a quick message as I step back inside, I ask Olive to come get me so we can jump my car. She's outside my house 15 minutes later, honking, with the top down on her convertible. She has her long hair braided tightly, keeping it out of her face, and she looks like a movie star in her oversized sunglasses.

She waves at something over my shoulder, and I steal a look at Ben's house. He's back outside weeding the planters and gives her a little wave back. He gives me a wolfish grin, and I can tell even from here that he's thinking about the way I grabbed him and kissed him. I compulsively suck my bottom lip between my teeth because now I'm thinking about it and this is *terrible* timing for damp panties. He watches me all the way to Olive's car, and there's way too much heat in his eyes for him to be thinking about that rhododendron.

"Hey," I say to Olive as I sink down into the passenger seat. Ben's eyes are back on his plants, but he's grinning broadly, dimples in full effect. Olive lifts her sunglasses to her forehead and gives me a mischievous grin. She pointedly looks at Ben and back to me, twice, before wiggling her eyebrows.

"Um, far be it from me to meddle, but what is up with you two?" This bitch isn't even whispering.

"Nothing," I say through clenched teeth. "Let's go."

Olive laughs quietly. "Nice try, Lilah. You're a shit liar. Do you know that? There is some sizzling tension between you two. I'm kind of afraid to be in the middle lest I get burned."

I groan quietly and hiss, "Come on, Olive. I mean it. Let's go."

Olive steps on the clutch and throws the car into reverse as she eyes me, one eyebrow raised, and lips pursed as she tries not to smile. "Why are you blushing like that? That doesn't look like nothing. If something happened with sexy Clark Kent, you are legally obligated to tell me."

"No, I'm really not. I keep telling you that the sister code isn't legally binding. Besides, nothing is happening." I never should have told her about him. I blame Sally and her tequila slinging. I was weakened by my hangover.

"How are things at the bakery this morning?" I ask her.

"Oh, hell no! You are not changing the subject. Nice try, though. Why was he giving you the I-want-to-do-bad-things-to-you eyes? And what the hell did you do to your forehead? I swear, you hurt yourself more than any person I have ever met."

I know her well enough to know she'll never let up unless I give her something. "Fine, he woke me up with the mower at 8 am after a shitty night. I fell out of bed and hit my head on my nightstand before stomping outside to yell at him. I didn't realize I was bleeding, so he took me inside and he bandaged me up," I say, pointing at my forehead, "because this was his fault. After that we had... a weird moment."

The light turns red and Olive eyes me hard, dropping her chin, rolling her eyes and making aggressive air quotes as she asks, "What exactly constitutes a weird moment? And side note, you've hit your head on that nightstand like three times now."

"Yeah, I kind of want to burn the thing into a pile of ash and melted hardware."

Olive laughs. "I'll help you. That nightstand is ugly as sin, and it clearly wants you dead. But don't change the subject. What was weird? Did he have a closet full of melted dolls? One of those maps on the wall with a bunch of strings connecting things? A room dedicated to his love of puppets?"

44

"Oh my god, no. At least I didn't see anything weird. No, his house is totally normal."

Olive glares at me over her sunglasses. She's not going to let this go. The sun warms my shoulders as I stare back at her, not wanting to give in to the silent treatment, but I can't stand it when she does that.

"You're like a dog with a bone, you know that? Fine. We were fighting, and... I kissed him. I lost my head for a minute. That's all."

Olive gives me a wide-eyed, surprised smile. "Have you ever made the first move before?"

"No, and I didn't make a move. I just... I got carried away for a second."

We pull into the bar parking lot and my sister parks her car facing the front of my Jeep. With the sun shining and spring in the air, this parking lot feels completely different.

My phone buzzes in my pocket before we can get out. The screen reads "Unknown", so I throw my phone into my purse with an annoyed huff and step out of the car.

Olive digs around in her trunk, looking for the jumper cables while I hop out and lift the hood of my Jeep. I throw my key in the ignition and turn it out of habit. The damn thing starts right up.

Olive pops her head over the top of her trunk with a confused look. "What the hell? I thought you said it was dead last night."

"It was." I'm just as confused as I stare at the dashboard. There are no warning lights. Nothing is flashing or smoking or looks like it's about to explode.

"It wasn't even turning over last night. I don't understand." Now I'm annoyed. A dead battery is one thing. I figured I just left the lights on or something. If it's randomly working and then not working, that's probably something worse, like wiring or gremlins.

"Well shit. Let's just take it to Asher and Lukas. They can sort it out for you."

She's right. Besides, Asher will peck at me like a hen if he finds out I had car trouble and didn't let him check it out. Olive follows me on the short drive to our brother's auto shop so I can drop it off before we head to the bakery.

When we pull in, Asher is standing in front of a vintage sports car with the hood popped, holding a thermos of coffee and yelling his head off at our younger brother.

"It sounds like shit! The throttle isn't right!"

Lukas is behind the wheel with the door open as he revs the engine.

"What?" Lukas yells from behind the wheel, still revving. I can tell, even from here, that he's fucking with Asher.

"I said it sounds like shit! The throttle is off!" Lukas cuts the engine mid-sentence, so Asher is suddenly screaming into the quiet morning air. Lukas chuckles as we walk over. Asher just rolls his eyes.

Olive's voice is dripping in playful sarcasm as she says, "You've *clearly* got the florker misaligned with the rigger."

"Twerp," Asher says as Lukas pulls her in and gives her an aggressive noogie.

She screams like a wounded bobcat and fights her way free. "Knock it off, dickbag!"

"Nah, I've gotta get it out of my system while Brooks isn't around. He doesn't let me give you noogies anymore."

"Oh really?" she replies sarcastically. "He doesn't want you giving his fiancée a noogie? How shocking! Maybe it's because we aren't eight years old anymore. Even though you still act like it."

Asher rolls his eyes again and interrupts before they can get into it some more. "What's up?" he asks me because I'm clearly the voice of reason in this menagerie.

"My Jeep wouldn't start last night but it fired right up this morning. I didn't even have to jump it. I have no idea what's wrong with it. Can you just

46

take a look at it?"

Asher gives it a thoughtful look. "That's odd. I put a new battery in it a couple months ago. Maybe a loose cable... I dunno. I'll figure it out. I'll drop it off at the bakery later."

"You're the best!" I tell him before hugging both my brothers and heading back to Olive's car.

Chapter 12: Lilah

We hit the side door of Olive Branch Bakery and a wave of delicious air hits us from the kitchen. The mixed-up aroma of sourdough baguettes, sugary cupcakes, buttery pastries and fresh coffee wash over me. I swear to god, even the air has calories in the bakery.

We scrub up, put on our chef coats and aprons, and get to work. The bakery is Olive's baby. She's the one who went to culinary school, and she's the one who runs day-to-day operations. Part of me loves working with her and not having to be in charge. I'd rather be the number two (or three) and have the freedom to do whatever else I want.

We have a light prep list of sugar flowers, baking a few cakes and whipping up a metric shit-ton of vanilla buttercream. We've been working ahead to make sure the bakery is fully stocked now that tourist season is creeping up on us.

Olive is hyper-focused for most of the morning, but once we get to the sugar flowers, she starts to relax a little. We tag-team them: I roll out the gum paste and cut the petals, Olive ruffles the edges and builds the flowers on their wires, hanging them to dry on the little rack in front of us.

We work quietly, and I can tell Olive is turning something over and over in her head. She drops a flower and swears as she throws it in the trash. She clears her throat. "In the spirit of honesty, I feel like I should tell you to give this Ben guy a chance."

I give her a quelling look. "He's all emotion-y. If it was just sex, I would have jumped his bones already, but he wants to date. He keeps trying to get to know me."

"Oh, heaven forbid!" Olive mocks me. "You know that I don't think most guys are worth the time or energy they require. But... I can tell you like him. You always assume things will go to shit, but maybe this guy is worth giving a shot. Not all men are deadbeats like Dad."

I snort derisively. "I know that. I just think it's stupid to date my neighbor. How can I avoid him when things go wrong?"

"Aha! See! You're doing it right now! Maybe just this once you can try dating someone without planning for the worst."

I want to be mad at my sister. I want to argue with her and tell her she's wrong, but there's a tiny niggling thought in the back of my brain when I think about the way Ben touched me. He kissed me like I was the air he needed to breathe. I can still feel his massive hand sliding up my bare thigh.

If I hadn't bolted out of his house, I could have spent the morning exploring his abs with my tongue instead of dealing with car trouble. But then I remember the way he made me tremble with need; the desperation he brought out in me. Ultimately, isn't that what makes him dangerous? Everything about him is addictive, and I have the distinct feeling that he would be nearly impossible to walk away from.

Olive waves a hand in front of my face. "Oh my god, don't fantasize about him right now! We were having a conversation!"

"I'm not!"

"You're a terrible liar. Anyway, Brooks and I want you to invite Ben to dinner at your house next week. You're already making us dinner, what's one more person?"

"Excuse me? You invited yourselves over for a housewarming dinner and I agreed to cook for the two of you, but I did *not* agree to host a double date in my new house. You can't just demand I invite Ben."

"It's more of a request than a demand," Olive says with a grin.

"No." I tell her. "Hard pass." I will not voluntarily create a situation where I have to fight down my unbearable sexual attraction to Ben while my sister and future brother-in-law watch.

"Lilah," a soft voice comes from the front of the kitchen. Allison, the barista, is poking her head around the corner. "Lukas is up front." She disappears and I sigh with relief as I strip off my gloves and toss them in the trash. I hate being without my Jeep.

Lukas is hanging out in the dining room of the cafe. It's late afternoon and the tables are mostly empty. I expect the big smiles Lukas usually has for me, but he's got a tight, worried look on his face and he's fidgeting with my keys. He tries to smile, but it just makes him look more pinched than before.

"That is not a good face," I try to tease him. I'm used to that look on Asher. He's the worrier, not Lukas.

"Hey Ladybug, can you come outside with me? I need you to look at this real quick."

Now I'm really worried. My brothers only use my nice nickname when something is really wrong. I follow him out front where he already has the hood up on my car.

"Look at this," he says, pointing at the battery posts and the cables connecting to them.

I put my hands on my hips and look at the battery like I know anything about cars. One of the benefits of having two mechanics for brothers is that I've never actually needed to learn anything about cars. I'm sure I'm capable and could learn but they've been happy to do every oil change, brake job and car repair I've needed. It also serves to fulfill Asher's need to look out for the rest of us. Who am I to take that away from him?

"Yes, I see," I say seriously. "Unless I'm mistaken, that appears to be a car battery."

Lukas rolls his eyes. "Don't be a smart ass," he says and points at the cables again. "Look right here. I replaced these last year because the old ones were corroded. Remember?" I nod, because it sounds familiar. "Did you mess with these cables at all?" he asks.

I am super confused. "No... we didn't even attach the jumper cables. It started up before we connected anything. Why?"

Lukas runs a hand through his long hair, his brows drawn together so hard it looks uncomfortable.

"You're stressing me out," I tell him. I give him a smack on the chest just to make my point.

50

"We use socket wrenches on these at the shop. Always. But there are gouges here that look like someone used a wrench or pliers or something on the bolts."

I look closer at the bolt Lukas is pointing at and there are, in fact, deep scratches in the metal. Loud buzzing fills my ears as I try to breathe and process what he's saying.

"You're saying you think someone tampered with my battery while I was working last night? That's what Asher thinks too?"

Lukas huffs out a worried breath. "Yeah. We both think so. And I think they reconnected it before you and Olive came back this morning, which doesn't lead me to believe it's just a prank. I think someone wanted to isolate you and get you into their car. It's easy with a Jeep, since they don't have to get inside the cab to pop the hood."

Lukas keeps running his hands through his hair, and it's standing up at weird angles. I'd laugh if I wasn't so busy trying to squash a panic attack. An icy ball of lead settles deep in my stomach. If this was anyone else telling me about the scratches, I'd laugh it off, but my brothers are meticulous about their work. If Lukas says someone tampered with my car, I believe him.

Suddenly the warmth of the spring sunshine doesn't feel like it's reaching my skin anymore. Someone wanted me stranded, alone in the dark outside the bar, at 3 am. What if my phone had died before I reached Luis? I have a flash of the car that pulled into the parking lot and turned around with their high beams cranked up, blinding me as I got into the safety of Luis' car.

For a second I think I might throw up. Did I come that close to danger?

"Asher thinks we should file a police report," Lukas says, interrupting my terrifying train of thought. "He's freaking out."

"And tell them what? That there are scratches on my battery cables? What are they going to do?" I ask him. "It's not even like they can dust for prints. It was pouring rain last night, and Olive and I had our hands all over the hood this morning before you even got to it. They won't take it seriously. Just document it in my car paperwork at the shop in case anything else happens."

Lukas looks like he wants to argue with me. But what's the point? He knows I'm right.

Chapter 13: Ben

"There's a present on its way to you," my sister says. I can hear honking in the background and then it sounds like she's holding the phone away from her ear as she yells, "It's a crosswalk, asshole! Pedestrians have the right of way!"

"Good morning to you too," I tease her back. The honking fades as she curses under her breath. "How's the festival? How is DC?"

"Wet and crowded. I'd give my Nikon 24-70 for a desert assignment right now."

"Only you could be salty about a cherry blossom festival."

"Yeah, well, you try getting a decent shot while thousands upon thousands of yokels swarm the tidal basin and the humidity defies science. I haven't had to drink water since I landed. I'm just absorbing it from the air like a frog." I laugh because that so perfectly sums up my sister. "How are Mom and Dad?" she asks.

"Enjoying early retirement. Mom is making wind chimes out of recycled trash and Dad is building a shed."

"Well, that sounds very... nice." Ella sounds like she'd rather stab herself in the neck with a rusty pipe than make wind chimes and build a shed.

"I think it is for them," I say. "They miss you. Mom thinks you're in India and can't get reception."

Ella laughs. "Yeah, sorry about that. I needed a break. She keeps asking if I've met anyone. She wants grandbabies and hasn't come to terms with the fact that you are her only hope."

"It's a bleak prospect."

"Surely there must be someone out there for you. You're so normal."

"Oh yeah, totally normal," I scoff. "Reclusive hacker screams normal."

"But you're a *rich,* reclusive hacker. You can get away with the rest because it's balanced out by your bank account. Speaking of *the rest,* thank you for helping my friend the other day."

She's being vague on purpose. We rarely talk about the people I help in my side work. Mostly because the fewer breadcrumbs we leave, the better. It's bad enough that Ella often has a physical connection to them.

"Piece of cake," I tell her.

There's a lengthy pause. I know she has something to get out, and she's struggling. I'm patient.

"It was bad," she finally says.

"How bad?" I ask.

"I'm not supposed to talk about it. Support groups are supposed to be anonymous."

"Well, technically she's a completely new person now. Does confidentiality apply when someone disappears off the face of the Earth? Besides, I can tell you need to talk about it and it's not like you can do that in a support group. I'm a vault, Ella. You know that."

My sister makes a choking sound. Shit, I made her cry.

"She turned up in a group out here all black and blue," she says through the tears. "She had handprint bruises on her arms and her face was still swollen. They locked him up, I mean they had plenty of evidence. But then he started calling her from prison. Sent letters. Threatened her over and over. Even from behind bars, he had someone trash her car and throw rocks through her windows. It wasn't going to end until one of them was dead."

A story she knows only too well. My sister survived her own abusive marriage, but some trauma never goes away. Much like the guilt I carry because I was too self-absorbed with my work to see what was happening with my sister.

"She's safe now, Ella." I try to calm her as much as I can, considering I'm on the far side of the country. "And so are you. We took care of her. She has a new life, and no one will ever know where she went."

54

"I know," she whispers.

"I miss you. Come out to California when you're done with D.C.," I tell her.

"Yeah, I'd like that. Maybe in the fall. How's the girl next door?" she asks, changing the subject. I can hear her voice is still shaking, but if she's ready to talk about something else, that's fine.

"Lilah? She's... a firecracker. I'm sure you'd like her."

"I bet I will," I can hear her smiling through the phone. "Does she know what you do?"

"Not yet," I hedge. "But I'll tell her. After I convince her to like me."

Ella laughs. She finally sounds like her normal happy self. "If anyone could do it, it's you. I've gotta run. Good luck with that."

"Have fun, be safe," I say.

"You too."

After hanging up, I check my watch. I'm supposed to be downtown to meet Jack for lunch in half an hour. I swear, if it wasn't for him, I'd never leave my house. It's not that I'm antisocial, exactly. I just have everything I need here. Well, almost everything. The pull I feel towards Lilah Donovan is almost frustrating in its intensity. It would be so much easier if I could just forget about her and go back to a world where all I think about is my computer.

Easier, but much less interesting.

I find Jack in the rooftop bar at the address he gave me. A pretty blond server is trying to flirt with him, batting her hand against his arm and fluttering her eyelashes. Jack looks bored. Jack always looks bored, but he's usually just deep in thought. I sit down next to him and pat his knee.

"Sorry I'm late, sweetheart," I say with my best apologetic face. The waitress gives me a wide-eyed look and disappears faster than a fox down a hole.

"Thanks for that," Jack says wryly.

"Oh, you weren't interested. Don't act like I didn't just save you."

"Oh, thank you for rescuing me from the big bad waitress," he says sarcastically. "She was terrifying, and I never could have chased her off on my own. Whatever would I do without my big protector?" He shoots me a sarcastic look. "I needed a date for a fundraiser next month. She would have been fine."

I want to ask him why he'd settle for "fine", but I know he won't give me a straight answer.

"How's your mom?" I ask instead.

"Widowhood doesn't seem to bother her. She's taking up pottery," he says.

"Perfect, she can open a roadside stand with my mom and her wind chimes," I say as I flag the bartender down. I order an iced tea and a cheeseburger. My dad would hate the cheeseburgers out here. Everything has avocado and expensive cheese, and nobody squishes the bun down in tin foil.

Jack takes a drink of his iced tea, crunching on an ice cube with a thoughtful expression on his face. He opens his mouth to say something, but we're both distracted by a chorus of laughter. I look over my shoulder at the group of women out on the deck, they're sitting on couches, sipping water and there's something oddly familiar about a couple of their faces. I'm trying to place them when the woman closest to me leans back, giving me a clear view of the woman behind her. The sight sends blood pumping furiously through my body, so strong that it's all I can hear or feel.

Lilah, in a white dress, her hair shimmering in the sunshine as she laughs at something an older woman with *incredibly* blue hair is saying. I don't think I've ever seen her look so happy. My chest constricts uncomfortably, and I realize I'm jealous. I want her to look at me like that.

Chapter 14: Lilah

I'm just putting the finishing touches on the lemon meringue tarts when someone sneaks up behind me, intentionally scaring the shit out of me. I let out a screech that could probably wake the dead and whip around to see my sister Julia laughing so hard she looks like she might pee herself. She's gripping the edge of the marble countertop and gasping for dear life.

"Gotchu... so good..." she says between cackles.

"Very mature, Julia. Now I have to make another batch of meringue just to redo two tarts."

"No, you don't," she says before swiping a tart with each hand. "You'll make us late for lunch. I'll just eat these and then it's like it never even happened." She takes a huge bite out of one. Olive walks back into the kitchen carrying an empty sheet tray.

"What in the fresh hell are you doing in my kitchen?!" she yells at Julia. "Your hair isn't even in a ponytail for Christ's sake! Get out!"

Julia laughs and skedaddles back out the side door, taking her ill-gotten gains with her.

"Animal!" Olive yells at her retreating back before shaking her head at me. "Did she mess those up on purpose?"

"Oh, for sure. You know how she is with lemon curd. She's practically a raccoon. You could always send her an invoice for them."

"Nah," Olive waves a hand in the air. "I'll just steal a nice bottle of wine next time I'm in her apartment. Ready for lunch?" she asks.

"Yup, let me put these in the display case and we can go."

"Hand them off to Allison. She needs something to do besides text her boyfriend." Olive rolls her eyes so hard I'm afraid she's going to pull a muscle. "At least she's peeled her eyeballs off of Brooks."

Olive, Julia, and I walk to Sally's boutique, enjoying the sunshine and clear blue sky. It's only a couple blocks and barely enough time for Julia to fill us in on how much she despises the doctors at the hospital. Sally waves at us from the front display where she's dusting a mannequin in a long black sequin sheath dress.

Sally's in her mid-60s and wild as all hell. Her hair is a shocking shade of turquoise and she's wearing flowing layers of white clothing and what might be every gold necklace and bracelet she carries in the shop. She kisses us each on the cheek as she ushers us inside. Styx is playing in the background as we spot Gran in the back admiring a lime green tunic. I swear to god; they cut Gran and Sally from the same cloth.

"I've got a present for you!" Sally singsongs as she hustles into the back room of the boutique.

"I have no idea which one of us she meant, but I call dibs," Julia spouts off.

Sally reappears a minute later with three dresses on hangers. "I just got these samples and they're in your sizes." She hands me a short white lace dress with a low v neck and long sleeves.

"Slutty bridal chic?" I ask her with a grin.

Sally rolls her eyes at me. "Just try it on before you snark at me about it. I guarantee that will look like a million bucks on you."

"My ass will hang out of this!" I tell her, but I scoot back to the dressing room. I can argue with Sally all day, but we'll never get to lunch if I don't at least try it on.

Olive and Julia follow me, and we change into our new dresses. Julia's dress is a red knee-length stretch jersey and clings to her every curve, making her look every inch like the pinup model she is. Olive's is a navy-blue linen sheath that makes her look like a modern Kennedy. Again, perfect.

I finally get the nerve to look at myself in the mirror. I'm shorter than both my sisters. I'm not as thin as Olive or as classically curvy as Julia. I'm more... athletic? I've always been a little insecure about it, but holy shit this dress is doing me every favor. My legs look incredible and even though I'm only 5'2", they look long as hell. I'm never taking this dress off, even if I

58

could wear it for a wedding on the Vegas Strip.

Sally throws the changing room curtain back and whistles at us. "Let's go! I'm starving." I toss my jeans and t-shirt into my oversized purse. Julia complains about being overdressed for lunch, but Sally shuts her down immediately.

"You can never be overdressed!"

"She should put that on her business cards," Julia mutters.

Olive snatches a card off the front desk as we walk by and hands it to Julia. "She did," she whispers with a grin.

Sally planned lunch this month and refused to tell us where we were going, so we follow her down Main Street on foot. I link arms with Gran, and she tells me all about her garden as we walk together. We get to a hotel and Sally opens the front door, gesturing grandly for us to enter. She marches us across the lobby to a bank of elevators.

"Are we having room service for lunch?" I tease her as we step inside.

"Ha-ha, very funny smartass." She grins back as she hits the button for the top floor. We step out into a rooftop restaurant covered with pergolas and potted trees.

"Holy shit..." Julia trails off. "How did I not know this was here?"

Sally just smirks and gives the hostess a name for the reservation. Not her name, of course.

"Sally Clooney?" Olive asks.

Sally sighs and puts a hand over her heart. "A woman has to have ambition, otherwise she stagnates." I can't help laughing at that.

We sit under a vine-covered pergola on outdoor sofas situated around a stone table. Vineyards cover the hills in the distance and when the wind blows my hair over my shoulder, I take a deep breath. I've never been more grateful to live in California than I am at this moment. Sally orders a round of mojitos when the server comes by and I groan.

"One drink, Sally. One! I'm never getting drunk with you again," I warn her.

"Oh, come on," Olive teases. "It's not her fault you can't hold your liquor and hit on Clark Hottie Kent next door." I smack her thigh, but the damage is already done. Gran is leaning in, mischief in her eyes, and Sally has an eyebrow firmly situated around her hairline.

"What?!" Julia gasps. "You didn't tell me about that!" she says accusingly.

I wince as I sip my water. "Yeah, not my finest moment," I say.

"Oh, I don't know. I thought it was kind of cute," comes a deep rumbly Texas twang behind me. Tingles run up my spine and my shoulders snap back with a little shiver.

Gran, Sally, and Julia are all staring somewhere behind me with their mouths gaping open. I turn slowly and sure enough, Ben is standing right there. I am suddenly *very* aware of the low neckline on this dress and the way the hem has crept all the way up my thighs. Great. Perfect. I'm fine. This is totally fine.

Except I'm still staring at Ben. And I don't think I can recover from this.

I don't have to do anything because he leans down and kisses me on the cheek in what I'm sure looks like a friendly gesture to everyone else. It happens so fast that I don't even register the touch until it's gone, leaving behind a warm tingle where his lips grazed my skin and the pounding of my heart as it tries to escape my chest.

"Ha-h" I stutter and swallow the lump in my throat. I collect myself and then say, "Hi. Hi, Ben." Oh yeah, I'm smooth as silk over here. If someone could dig a hole for me to crawl into, that would be great.

Ben gestures to a man sitting at the bar. "I'm having lunch with my friend, Jack." I glance over and his friend waves at me with a half-interested smile. He has dark eyes and short dark hair and he's wearing an expensive suit. Something about him gives off a devil-may-care attitude. Give him a hat and an earring and he'd make an excellent pirate.

Sally mutters, "Yes please," under her breath and Olive nearly chokes on her drink.

Ben waves back to his friend like nothing happened and continues, "I saw you and couldn't pass up the chance to come say hi. Since you won't let me take you out, and all." His adorable half-smirk lifts one side of his mouth. Despite the cocky smile, there's a vulnerability in his eyes that is stirring up some emotions I'm not totally comfortable dealing with.

Ok, maybe I kind of regret running out of his house like a complete chicken the other day. I'd be lying if I said I hadn't been thinking about that kiss 24/7.

I drop my gaze... and realize I'm at eye level with his dick. Even in the pale tan chino shorts he's sporting, it's hard to hide what he's packing. Pun intended, because I am a child.

Trying to regain some control of the situation, I stand and smooth my dress down my legs as far as it will go. Damn Sally and her free dress temptations. If I was still wearing my jeans and t-shirt, I might feel a little less naked, both figuratively and literally. Although... it's hard to miss the appreciative way Ben looks me up and down; and when he bites his lip, I have to admit, I'm not mad at it.

"Ben, these are my sisters, Olive and Julia, my grandmother, and our friend, Sally." I've finally got my voice back, even if it is a little breathy and quavery. I look back at them, desperately willing Sally to behave as I say, "Everyone, this is my neighbor, Ben."

Ben steps around the edge of the sofa, shaking everyone's hand and doling out million-watt smiles. "I won't keep you from your lunch. Nice to meet you, ladies. Lilah..."

My name rolls off his tongue like liquid sex before he lets his voice trail off, the pause pregnant with promises. An empty second that says a million things. A micro-moment dripping with how much he wants me and an oath that he hasn't given up on me. Time stands still for a split second, nothing moving except for the breath in my chest and a slow blink.

And then he winks at me, turns, and heads back for the bar, leaving me frozen in his wake. I watch him walk away for far too long before plopping back on the sofa and exhaling roughly.

I almost forgot I wasn't alone until Julia whistles low and leans across the table with a serious expression on her face.

"Lilah, we need to get a shitload of pregnancy tests because I think every woman in this bar just ovulated."

Chapter 15: Ben

It nearly kills me not to look back at Lilah as I rejoin Jack at the bar, and I make it at least 75% of the way before I give in. She's sitting down again and laughing at something her sister said.

"That's the bartender from Blue Ruin, right?" Jack eyes Lilah appreciatively, and I have the sudden impulse to punch my best friend in the face. I hold back, settling for flexing my fist and clenching my jaw.

"Yeah, and her sisters."

"Jesus, those are some good genes," he says. "They look so familiar. I feel like I know them from somewhere."

I've resisted the urge to poke into Lilah's family online. Normally, I wouldn't think twice about it. Hell, I've dodged plenty of bullets with good old-fashioned googling. If someone puts something on the internet, I figure it's fair game... but not with Lilah. If I learn something about her, I want it to be because she tells me herself. She's a challenge and a half, though I feel like I'm finally getting somewhere. I didn't miss the dazed expression when I kissed her cheek or the soft look in her eyes before I walked away.

Jack snaps his fingers, pulling me out of my thoughts. "Do they have two brothers? Dark hair, run Donovan Auto?"

"Yes to the brothers, though I'm not sure about the auto shop."

"They worked on my bike; do you remember? You picked me up there once."

"Vaguely? You want me to introduce you? Sally, the lady with blue hair sounded interested."

Jack gives her a thoughtful look. "Pity I'm not into cougars."

"I wasn't aware you had a type. Your dating life seems more like a free-for-all."

Jack flips me off half-heartedly. "Don't be a dick. Of course I have a type, I just don't like to limit myself."

"That's fine, as long as you don't end up with another Daphne situation."

Jack makes the sign of the cross. "Do you mind? Say her name twice more and you'll summon her."

"Sorry," I say with a laugh. Jack lost his dad last year and his money-grubbing ex-fiancé left him when he left his lucrative job in San Francisco to take over the crumbling family winery. I can't fault him for having a little fun with his freedom, even if I wouldn't do the same thing.

We spend the rest of lunch talking about the winery. I do my damnedest not to watch Lilah smiling and laughing in the sunshine, but it's difficult. I'm like a moth to the flame with her.

Lilah gets up to leave as Jack and I are waiting for our check. The patient, strategic side of me knows I should play it cool, let her leave with just a wave or nod. She looks at me as her group heads for the elevator, and I can't help winking at her as I look her up and down one last time. She's sexy as hell, a small smile playing at the corner of her lips despite a solid effort to hide it.

Fuck strategic.

I dig in my wallet for cash and slap a fifty on the counter before smacking Jack on the back. "Good to see you, man," I say before hopping off the bar stool and bolting for the bank of elevators.

Lilah is gone by the time I get there. I press the button and wait, tapping my fingers against my thigh. But none of the doors open and time is slipping away, every second putting more distance between us. I spin and find the door for the stairs, running down them two at a time until I hit the lobby. I catch a flash of white lace and tan legs walking out the front door and jog to catch up.

The sidewalks are crowded with the first rush of spring tourists, drawn downtown for lunch and shopping. I have to weave through a group of Red Hat ladies, excusing myself as I go. They titter and one of them catcalls me, or at least I think it passes for a catcall. What else would you call it when a grandma says, "Hey sugar, where are you headed?" before slapping my ass? Wine country is weird.

64

Between the handsy septuagenarian and the sight of Lilah, just 10 feet ahead of me, I'm so distracted that I accidentally bump right into a man.

"Sorry," I tell him without taking my eyes off my girl. The man just grunts and heads into a shop, ignoring me. Whatever. Lilah must have heard the commotion because she stops walking, turns, and locks eyes with me.

"Let me guess, you're walking this way?" she asks with an arched eyebrow.

"Crazy, huh?" I say with a grin. She bites her lip, clearly not buying it, but she waits for me to catch up. We fall into step behind her sisters who both turn, giving me identical, appraising looks, clearly judging whether I'm good enough for Lilah. Neither seems to find me lacking, but I don't miss the communicative look they give each other. I get the distinct impression that the women in this family are not to be messed with.

The other women peel off towards a shop. Olive tells Lilah she needs to grab something and will meet her back at the bakery in a few minutes. It feels like a thinly veiled attempt to leave me and Lilah alone, but I'm sure as fuck not complaining.

"Oh. Ok..." Lilah replies. She looks down the street and then gives me an embarrassed smile.

"Where are you headed?" I ask Lilah.

"Back to work," she says, gesturing at a red clapboard building two blocks down.

She's so close that I can smell her strawberry scented shampoo on the air and when we shift to let someone walk by, I place my hand on her lower back to pull her closer. Instead of pulling away, she leans just a bit closer into my side.

"Day job?" I ask.

Lilah nods. "Only job, actually. I quit the bar. Olive owns the bakery; I help her out and I'm taking over the coffee roasting."

"In that?" I ask again, sweeping my eyes over her dress and the long stretches of exposed skin. She looks at me out of the corner of her eye and I don't miss the smile that keeps creeping higher on her face.

Lilah laughs and pats her bag. "God no. I'm changing back into my jeans. I couldn't bake in this."

The image of her bending over to pull something out of the oven in that little dress grips me and I desperately try to pull up the least sexy images I can think of... *Baseball. My grandmother. Hitler in a thong.*

My fingers inadvertently flex against her spine as we approach the red building, the only tell my body gives at the thought of letting her go. A sign reading "Olive Branch Bakery" hangs over the door.

I contemplate tossing her over my shoulder and convincing her to spend the rest of the day with me, but I'm a gentleman to the core, so I step ahead and hold the door open for her instead. She pauses before heading inside and her lips part and then shut again like she can't decide what to say to me.

She finally settles on, "Thanks for the company."

"Anytime," I reply as she ducks inside, leaving me alone on the front porch.

Chapter 16: Lilah

I spend the entire day cooking and cleaning up my house to get ready for dinner with Olive and Brooks. I finally got the last of my boxes unpacked and my books neatly organized on the shelves in my living room.

I'm putting the finishing touches on dinner and dancing to music in the kitchen while I wait for Olive and Brooks to arrive. They were supposed to be here five minutes ago, but that's just Olive in a fucking nutshell. It drives Brooks crazy to be late everywhere they go, but he loves her too much to complain. Much.

I sprinkle some grated parmesan and chopped parsley on top of the pasta, pull the roasted chicken out of the oven, and add butter to the pan of asparagus sizzling on the stovetop. Everything is perfect. This might be the best meal I've ever made in my life, and if my sister doesn't hurry her ass up, I'm going to start without her.

After checking that the coconut panna cotta in the fridge has fully set, I pull out my phone to check on my sister. This is why we have Find My iPhone turned on. Spying on each other's location is Sister 101 as far as I'm concerned, but before I even get the app open, the doorbell rings. Finally.

I try to untie my apron as I walk to the door, but the damn waist tie is frayed and tangled. I try twisting it sideways so I can free myself as I open the front door. I'm still peering around my hip to see where the snag is when I say, "You're going to have to help me out of this thing, sweet tits."

"Gladly," comes a deep male rumble.

"Fuck!" I yell as I stumble backwards in surprise. Standing in the place where I expected to see my sister is none other than Benjamin Fucking Clark.

"Jesus! You scared the shit out of me!" I clutch my chest and wheeze at him. He's wearing jeans and a lightweight gray sweater. All I can see is his broad chest and muscled shoulders outlined in the knit pattern. Holy god, he looks so good. Why does he always have to look so good? My panties shouldn't get wet just because he's walking around in a sweater, but couldn't he wear sweatpants or something?

Scratch that. If I saw him strolling around in gray sweats, I probably couldn't stop myself from jumping his bones. Socks with sandals. That might be the only thing he'd look bad in.

Ben is smiling at me with an eyebrow cocked like he doesn't understand why I'm surprised. "Dinner smells amazing. Can I give you a hand with anything?" he asks, gesturing behind me.

"What?" I ask, thoroughly confused. "No. Dinner is ready but... can I help you with something?"

Ben flashes me a crooked grin and squints at me like I've lost my mind.

"Do I have the wrong night or something?" He asks. "I may be a Southern boy, but I'm not as slow as I sound," he says, drawing a card out of his back pocket and showing it to me. I snatch the card out of his hand. No, not a card. An invitation. An invitation to a housewarming party. At my house. Tonight.

"What the fuck? Where did you get this?!" I ask him. My already pounding heart picks up with indignation because, even as I ask, I know.

"It was in my mailbox this afternoon. Kinda short notice, don't you think?" Ben jokes, his brown eyes flashing with mischief.

"Olive," I say flatly.

"Sure, I'd like an olive, I guess. Aren't you going to invite me in? Or is dinner on the front porch?" Ben is giving me an infuriatingly cocky look. I should hate it. If he was any other guy, I definitely would.

"No, I'm not offering you an olive. My sister. My sister did this." Even as I say it, my phone starts dinging with text messages in my front apron pocket.

Olive: Enjoy your date. P.S. Payback's a bitch!

Olive: Sorry I said bitch.

Olive: Please save a panna cotta for Brooks and me.

68

"Oh-ho-no!" I hiss at my phone. "No panna cotta for you!"

Ben is staring at me with a look somewhere in the crossroads of "she's lost her damn mind" and "oh my god, look how cute she is." It's then that I notice he's holding a gift bag, a bottle of wine and a head of romaine lettuce. I'm trying to ignore the way he smells like fresh laundry and cologne, even though it's making me a little weak in the knees.

"What's the lettuce for?" I ask. Ben takes a step towards me on the porch. I'm still one step higher than him, and it puts me at eye level with him. He's so close I can see little shots of gold and black running through his irises as he watches me, smiling that crooked smirk of his. It makes him look arrogant. Arrogant and insanely sexy.

"I'm guessing you didn't invite me over tonight," Ben says. He's so near that my skin is tingling, begging me to lean just another inch or two closer.

"No," I reply. Why do I sound so breathy? A better question might be, why can't I breathe right around him?

"Do you want me to leave?" he asks. I hesitate, not because I want him gone, but because I want him to stay so desperately. It makes me physically ache to think of sending him away, but he reads my hesitation the wrong way, giving me a rueful smile as he steps back and hands me the things he was carrying.

"Maybe another time," he says as he turns to go, his hands tucked in his pockets. All it takes is one glimpse of his broad back and the memory of the way he kissed me to make me move.

"No," I call out.

Ben turns, still wearing that wary, resigned smile. "No, not another time?"

I swallow my anxiety, "N-no, I don't want you to leave." I stutter and blush, my heart beating erratically. Reckless! Risky! It thunders in my chest. *Woman up*, I chastise myself.

"It's just... I made all this food. My sister and her fiancé were supposed to come over for dinner but... well, clearly, she's not coming. Do you like roasted chicken?"

Ben's face lights up like a kid on Christmas, and I've never seen anything so endearing. "Yes, ma'am. I love it." His ever-present smirk and dimples reappear as he walks back towards me. It's only after he steps inside that I realize I'm holding my breath and let it out in a soft whoosh as I close the door behind him. I can't believe Olive did this to me. A quiet voice in the back of my head whispers *Not to me. For me.*

Ben is standing in the entryway, rubbing his hands together and looking around.

"Yeah, it's... kind of empty," I apologize. I have one couch in the living room, a small table with four chairs in the dining room and not much else. I lick my lips, painfully nervous at what he might be thinking. "I've never lived alone before, so I don't have enough stuff to fill a house."

Ben grins at me. "I like it," he drawls. "It's uncluttered."

I let out a relieved laugh. "It is definitely that." I lead him into the dining room and set down the wine and gift bag on the table. I'm itching to open them both, but my curiosity is outweighing everything else.

"Ben, what's with the lettuce?" I ask.

He fights back a chuckle as he takes it from my hands, his fingers brushing mine. "It's for Frankie. I read that tortoises love romaine. I figured it was only fair I bring her a housewarming gift too."

My mouth hangs half open and I blink at him as I process what he just said. "You- you brought my tortoise a present?"

"Yes, ma'am."

"That might be the sweetest thing I've ever heard."

"I aim to impress," he replies. He's moved closer. Or maybe that was me? It's like he's lined his pockets with magnets and he's drawing me in so slowly I don't notice until I'm lost in the smell of him.

Shaking myself back to my senses, I ask, "Do you want to feed that to her? It's cute as hell when she gets going on something she likes." Ben eyes

70

me appreciatively as his smile grows even larger.

Chapter 17: Ben

"I would like that very much. Lead the way to the tortoise," I say.

Lilah grins nervously at me and fidgets on her feet. She seems determined to fight it, but I didn't miss the way she leaned towards me, clearly as drawn to me as I am to her. She's a skittish thing, but I grin to myself as I realize that I'm starting to win her over.

Lilah seems to have forgotten that she's still trapped in her apron. It's covered in llamas and cacti and makes her look fucking adorable. She turns and leads me through her living room to the back door. I need something to hold on to because the sight of her ass wrapped up in a black stretch dress is almost more than I can take. Somebody is going to have to wipe the drool off my chin after they restart my heart.

We stop in front of a wire enclosure with rocks and a happy-looking reptile chilling under a heat lamp. Lilah waves a hand at it. "Just pop it in there. She's greedy."

We watch for a minute as the tortoise chugs her way towards the greens and munches it with the most Zen expression I've ever seen on a living creature. How can such a bizarre little reptile be so... cute? I'd probably lose my man card if I openly gushed over a tortoise, but damn is she adorable.

Lilah must have remembered the apron because she starts fidgeting with the ties, trying to undo the knot again.

"I thought that was my job," I tease as I grab her hips and spin her around. She squeaks but holds still, letting me work at the ties. One of them is frayed and so tangled that I don't see how she could have only been wearing it a couple hours. It's taking far too long to free her because I'm so distracted. The scent of her strawberry shampoo keeps wafting up into my face, making me desperate to bury my face in her neck and breathe her in. Let's not even get into the way her dress hugs her hips and ass as she stands there still as a doe in the wood.

My fingers keep grazing her spine and I can't help enjoying the way she shivers at my touch, leaning back into me. It's probably subconscious, because I seriously doubt that I'll ever be able to get her to confess that she actually likes me.

She pulls her hair over one side and looks over her shoulder at me, giving me a long view down the front of her dress. "You can just cut it off if you have to," she says, her voice a husky whisper. It's my turn to shiver because holy damn, all I can see, hear and smell is Lilah and now I'm picturing myself cutting her dress and panties off her body after I finish with the apron. Because sure, why not? Maybe she's stuck in those too.

"Do you want scissors?" she asks, eyes wide and innocent. There's no way she knows the dirty thoughts running through my head right now. Yes, I want scissors. Or even better, I want to rip this ridiculous apron off her body with my bare hands, followed by every stitch of clothing she's wearing.

I pause for a second, just so she'll keep looking up at me like that. "I think I've almost got it, but scissors would be faster."

I follow her back to the kitchen, desperately hanging onto the last scrap of gentlemanly behavior I have left. She pulls scissors out of a drawer and hands them to me, eyeing me carefully before turning around.

"Still not a serial killer," I promise as I take them. I make quick work of the strap and reach around her to set them down on the counter. Lilah lifts the apron over her neck and turns, her body inches from mine, backside pressed against the counter. This feels awfully familiar. My dick is stirring, and at this point I'm fairly sure it's a Pavlovian response to having Lilah near me in a kitchen. She doesn't seem to be in any hurry to move as she watches me, bright green eyes piercing.

She doesn't flinch or pull away when I run a finger up her arm, smooth skin gliding under mine. I lean down, placing my hands on the counter, caging her in before I put my lips next to her ear and breathe her in. She trembles against me, her breathing faster and deeper than normal, like she's trying to maintain control. That won't do.

"I've been thinking about you," I tell her quietly as I brush my nose against the shell of her ear.

"Have you?" she whispers back.

I let my lips trace the side of her neck, loving the way little goosebumps pop up on her skin. No matter how hard she tries to deny it, her body was made for mine. No one can fight this kind of attraction, especially me. Not that I want to. My mind races with the dirty things I'd like to do to her, but I move slowly, taking my time as I kiss the tender skin below her ear.

"I can't seem to *stop* thinking about you," I whisper as my lips graze her neck. Lilah practically purrs against me as her hands slowly move over my biceps and chest in soft exploratory touches. The combination of her sweet cinnamon skin and silky soft hair is doing dangerous things to me. I couldn't resist her if I tried.

"What do you think about?" Her soft breath fans over my collarbone, sending tingles across my skin.

I groan softly. "If I told you every filthy thought I've been having, you might just run for the hills, and I'm not trying to scare you off, Princess," I whisper.

Lilah leans back to look up at me with a little scowl. The motion arches her back and does breathtaking things to the front of her dress. It's all I can do not to groan out loud. "I'm not a princess. I'm a grown-ass woman. Don't patronize me."

Even the defiance that flashes across her face can't disguise the lust in her hooded eyes, and the spark of temper does nothing to abate the need pulsing through my body. If anything, the way she challenges me turns me on even more.

She wants to hear it?

Alright, then.

Slipping my hand to the small of her back, I pull her soft curves into me, letting her feel every inch of her effect on my libido. She exhales roughly and pulls her bottom lip between her teeth as her eyes grow wider.

"I think about unzipping your dress and peeling you out of it. Slowly." I run a finger up her back to emphasize my point and she lets out a little shiver.

74

"I think about the way your legs felt wrapped around me when we kissed. I picture you naked. In my bed, in my shower, bent over the kitchen counter. I remember the way you taste, the sounds you make when you like what I'm doing... and I wonder what it would take to make you scream in bed." I nip her neck, eliciting a small moan. "I think about setting you on this counter and picking up where we left off. Mostly I think about kissing you, sinking into your tight pussy, and making you so needy you beg me to let you come."

She pulls her head back and looks at me, defiance and lust battling for control in her narrowed eyes. "I would never beg for it. I could just do it myself."

With a groan, I pull her hair into a ponytail, tilting her head farther back, watching the desire in her gaze win as I tell her the truth. "And I would beg you to let me watch."

Color flushes her cheeks. She wets her lips before saying, "Anyone ever tell you how dirty you are?" Her voice is breathy and rolls over me like silk. Her shallow, rapid breathing is causing her chest to rise and fall, brushing against my rib cage. She's trying to sound indignant, but lust is curled around every word as they tumble from her lips. She may think I'm dirty, but she obviously loves it.

"That's just the tip of the iceberg," I tell her, trying not to grin like a cocky bastard.

Chapter 18: Lilah

Holy shit. No one has ever spoken to me like that. Not even in a text message. I should *not* like it. It should offend me, right? I should slap him or throw a glass of ice water on him, but I don't have a glass of water handy and it would be a crime against humanity to mess up a face like that.

And maybe, just maybe, I like it a little. And maybe I *really* like the way he looks at me. His cocky smile is back, but the look in his eyes is pure sin. I suddenly have no doubt that this man could make me scream in bed.

If you had asked me a week ago, I would have told you that chemistry like this was a myth. A way to sell Hallmark movies and romance novels. But this intense attraction to one specific person is entirely new and, if I'm honest, scaring the shit out of me.

I never understood why other girls would get so boy-crazy or why my sister went so cuckoo-bananas over Brooks. Don't get me wrong, I think sex is great. Everyone needs to blow off some steam and a quick hook up is usually effective, even if the orgasms are lackluster. But I get it now. All I want in the world is to rip Ben's clothes off and lick him like a lollipop.

I wet my lips as I try to put together a response in my lust-addled brain. "This dress doesn't have a zipper," I mumble.

Oh, fuck me and my mouth. Why did I say *that*? In the entire lexicon of sexy things I could have responded with, why the hell did my mouth go with that one?

Ben's dimple pops as his grin spreads across his stupidly handsome face. From the tousled hair to the dimples and crooked smile, to, well, everything about his body, he's like my own personal kryptonite in a man suit. He literally melts my panties.

"I think I could figure something out," he says as he brushes the backs of his fingers up my side, grazing my ribs and the sides of my breast. It's all I can do to stifle the whimper trying to escape my lips.

"I bet you could." That's all the invitation he needs. The next thing I know, he's tunneling his fingers into my hair, cupping my head in his massive hand as he leans down to kiss me, fire burning in his eyes. He's so intense that I half expect him to maul me, but his lips are gentle as he presses them to mine. His thumb strokes my cheek as he pulls my lower lip between his teeth, grazing it sweetly before sweeping his tongue over it.

God, it's so good. He's so good. He takes charge of the kiss, holding my head where he wants it as his tongue sweeps into my mouth, tasting me and teasing me. His enormous body is pressing me into the countertop, half holding me up as I surrender to his touch. His hard length pulses against my belly and lust is winning out over good sense.

I'm gripping his shoulders like a life preserver in a stormy sea. If he stepped back, I'm afraid I would melt to the floor in a boneless heap. Maybe he can tell the effect he's having on my motor control, or maybe he just wants me higher because he scoops me up and deposits me on the counter, just like he did in his own kitchen. A lusty growl slips past his lips as he grabs my knees and spreads them, stepping between them. His hands slip up my thighs and under my dress to grip my ass and pull me closer as his tongue strokes against mine, claiming my mouth and sending hot waves of lust through my body. I can't fight the need to be closer to him anymore than I could stop a train barreling down its tracks.

My hips move against him desperately, seeking contact and friction and I can feel his steel length when I rock against him. He swallows my moan and kisses me breathless. I let my hands trail down his sweater and slip underneath to his tight, flat stomach. The contact makes him suck in a sharp breath, and I'm inordinately pleased to know I'm not the only one who is so affected by this. My fingers skate over his abs through the light sprinkle of hair trailing downwards from his belly button.

Ben's hand slips over my hip and lower stomach, teasing the edges of my panties. His touches are feather soft and I'm so overwhelmed and desperate for him to touch me, I very nearly say "please" out loud. But that's what he wants, and I can't make it that easy. I smile into the kiss and feel his lips pull up with mine. He knows exactly what he's doing to me.

He skims a finger over my sex and the sensation of his skin slipping over my panties is almost more than I can bear. He pets me and I gasp against his lips, spreading my legs wider to give him as much room as possible. His fingers sneak under the waistband of my panties and one digit slides between my folds.

Ben growls, cursing under his breath as he presses his forehead to mine. "You're so damn wet." His voice is ragged, and he's shaking like his control is stretched to its limits. I can't put words together, only gasp as he slips a finger deep inside me, his thumb gently pressing on my clit. I wrap my arms around his neck, clinging to him. Our breaths mix as he strokes in and out of me until I'm stretched tighter than a bowstring.

"Lilah," he grunts my name and I open my eyes, meeting his hungry look. It's too much, too intimate, and too intense, but it pushes me over the edge, and I come, my body releasing every last bit of tension in a wave of pleasure.

I let my forehead drop to his shoulder as my body goes slack. I reach down and fumble with his belt before I've even thought it through. I just need him in less clothing. I've got it halfway undone when Ben grabs my wrists. He's not rough, but his grip is firm as he holds both of my hands in one of his.

He lifts my chin gently, tilting my face to look up at him. His eyes hold mine so completely that I couldn't look away if I wanted to. I swear, something tangible passes between us. I'm confused about why he stopped me, but I can tell from the pained look on his face that it's killing him at least as much as it's bothering me.

"You are so beautiful," Ben whispers reverently as he strokes a thumb over my lower lip, before kissing me again. "I'll make you a deal. If you sit and have dinner with me, you can steal my belt buckle, my pants, and anything else you want."

My mouth is hanging open as I try to process what he's saying. I want him so badly. Nothing has ever felt so right.

"You're telling me that getting into your pants is contingent on us eating dinner together first."

78

Ben smirks, dimples on full display. "Yes, ma'am."

"This feels really backwards. You must really like roasted chicken." Even as I say it, I know I sound a little defensive.

Ben cups my jaw with both hands and kisses me sweetly. "I'm sure your chicken is great, but I've been trying to get to know you and this is the first chance you've really given me."

I cock my head to the side and open my mouth to argue, but he's not wrong. I can have one dinner with him and then I can sleep with him and get him out of my system... That always works the way it's supposed to, right? He's probably not even super likable once you get to know him.

Yeah... I don't know why I'm trying to lie to myself either.

Chapter 19: Ben

Even as the words leave my mouth, the entire lower half of my body screams in frustration. I'd have given almost anything to keep going. To let her take off my pants and wrap her hands around my cock. To pull that dress over her head and carry her ass to the bedroom.

But more than anything, I don't want this to be a one-time thing. I still don't understand what draws me to her so strongly, but I've never felt anything like it before and I'm damn sure going to do everything in my power to ensure I get to keep it. I genuinely want to get to know Lilah and if that means I have to give myself a case of blue balls, then so be it.

Lilah gets plates out of the cabinet and puts a whole chicken on a serving dish while I set the side dishes on the table. She directs me to a bottle of white wine in the fridge and I open it, pouring two glasses. I'm more of a beer guy, but you can't live in Sonoma without picking up a passing appreciation for a good chardonnay. Just don't tell my dad.

I pull Lilah's chair out for her and wait for her to sit down. My mother (figuratively) beat good manners into me, and she'd be appalled if I did any less. Lilah squints at me as I push her seat in, like she can't figure me out.

"Something wrong?" I ask her with a grin as I sit down next to her instead of across the table where she put my plate. I pull it over in front of me and let her pile food on it for me.

"Nope. I'm just trying to figure you out. You go from dirty talk to Southern gentleman in, like, the blink of an eye. You know that, right?"

She should hear my inner dialogue, it's still dirty talking her. It's also dirty talking her cooking skills. I try not to moan out loud when I bite into the chicken on my plate, but I can't stop myself once I hit the pasta.

"Hungry?" she teases.

"Always. But this is the best meal I've ever had."

Lilah blushes but takes the compliment. A trait I already love in her.
80

"So, what do you do?" she asks, breaking the silence. "I know you said you work from home."

"Cyber security," I tell her after a beat of hesitation. That's only a part of what I do, and it feels wrong to leave out the rest, even if it's still too soon to tell her about it. Lilah's eyes narrow as if cataloging my hesitation.

"What does that entail, exactly?"

"I test online systems for weaknesses. Mostly I find backdoors that other programmers might have left behind, or holes in security that someone else was too lazy to fix. Occasionally, I run phishing simulations for large corporations so they can identify employees that might be weak links. Once in a while I get to track down leaks and corporate spies. Those are the fun ones."

"Not to be pushy, but how do you get into that kind of work?"

"Do you want the nice version or the real version?" I ask her.

Lilah purses those pink lips at me like she can't believe I'd even ask.

"The real one, huh?" I sigh dramatically. "First, you have to understand that I was a reckless kid. I crashed my bike so many times my dad couldn't fix it anymore. I jumped off the town bridge into the river on a dare and got into fights with kids twice my size. Pre-growth spurt, obviously."

Lilah's lips twitch up in a smile, like she's imagining a scrappy little version of me. She's so magnetic, I just want to tell her everything, including the parts I can't.

"My dad started teaching me to code when I was nine, mostly as a way to keep me out of trouble. I took to it like a duck takes to water. I'm dyslexic, so reading and writing were hard for me. But as it turns out, my brain works a lot like a computer. I built my first computer when I was 10, started building webpages, even worked on a video game for a while. But eventually I got bored and went looking for more exciting things to do..."

She's watching me with so much quiet curiosity and despite my hesitation she gives me a little nod, raising her eyebrows as if to say, "Go on."

I clear my throat. "Well, I hacked the FBI when I was 17. It was stupid and impulsive... and I got caught. Six FBI agents showed up in tactical gear within the hour. They broke down the front door and scared the shit out of my sister and parents. God, my mom was so pissed."

"Did they arrest you?" Lilah has both elbows propped on the table, chin in her hands as she listens intently.

"Nope. They gave me a deal. They put me in a training program, and I had to work for them for five years. In exchange, I didn't have to go to Federal prison. I did my five years, buried my head in my work, and when it was over, I left to pursue work in the private sector." And help my sister pick up the pieces of her broken life, though I don't say that out loud.

I don't know what reaction I was expecting from her, but laughter isn't it. She chuckles softly with a look that I can only identify as relief.

"Why are you laughing?" I ask.

She looks up at me with her big green eyes. "Because you might be the first person I've ever met with a childhood more dramatic than mine. I mean, my brother Lukas got into a few scrapes with the law and we had a messed-up childhood but none of us hacked the FBI and lived to tell about it."

Lilah takes a deep breath in and holds it for a second before making her mind up about something and exhaling. "In the interest of honesty, my Gran raised me and my siblings. Mom and grandpa died in a car accident and my dad decided he didn't want to deal with five kids on his own, so he dropped us off with Gran and never came back."

"Jesus Christ."

"Yeah, my dad was kind of the worst, but I don't remember much about him. Olive and Asher are older, and they remember more. He wanted Gran to give him access to our trust funds, and when she said no, he took off." She scrunches her mouth to one side in a heartbreakingly adorable scowl. "Sorry. This got heavy really fast," she laughs softly.

I shrug and take her hand, "I'm glad you told me."

Lilah gives me a wobbly smile. "Me too." She opens her mouth to say something, but her phone vibrates on the counter behind her and she stands to grab it. Her dress gets hung up on her legs as she stands, I'm treated to the sight of her sexy-as-hell thighs. It's all I can do to keep my hands to myself.

She frowns at the screen. "Something wrong?" I ask as I try to ignore the way my pants are fitting too tight in the fly area.

"No, it's fine. I just keep getting these calls that say, 'Unknown Number.' I'm sure it's just a scam or telemarketer or something, but it's so annoying."

"I can look into that for you," I tell her with a grin.

She flashes me a megawatt smile as she gets two little jars out of something white out of the fridge. "Ooh, you might be handy to have around."

"Oh, I promise you I am very good with my hands," I tease back.

Lilah blushes so hard I wonder if I should be worried about her combusting. She sets one of the jars in front of me with a tiny spoon.

"Is that vanilla pudding?" I ask her. I haven't had vanilla pudding since I was a kid, but I used to love it.

"Excuse you, sir!" she says in mock-outrage as she tops the contents of the jar with a thick yellow sauce and sprinkles little cookie looking pieces on top.

"*That* is coconut panna cotta with passion fruit curd and brown-butter coconut shortbread."

Now it's my turn to let my mouth hang open. "I don't know what half of that means, but you had me at coconut."

Lilah grins at me as she sits back down and takes a small bite of the dessert. "Can I ask you something?" She doesn't lift her eyes as she says it.

"Anything," I tell her as I scoop up a spoonful of the stuff in the jar and take a bite. "Holy sh- I mean, that is really good."

Lilah laughs and takes another tiny bite. "You can swear, it doesn't bother me. My whole family swears like a crew of drunken sailors. You should hear my grandmother. Were you really mowing in the morning just to push my buttons?"

"Not at first. But you really are adorable when you're mad... I'm sorry, I can't help it!" I hold up my hands in mock surrender as she scowls at me. "Like right now. Your eyebrows scrunch up, your lips get all pouty and your eyes turn fiery. It's sexy as hell." I gesture at the front of my jeans where my dick is straining the tensile strength of my jeans.

She tries not to smile, but I can tell she likes the effect she has on me.

"My turn," I tell her. "Why do you keep turning me down?"

Chapter 20: Lilah

Oh boy. If I'm being honest, that's a question with a really long, in-depth answer. I pour myself a second glass of wine and top up Ben's. Liquid courage for the win.

"I don't date," I say before taking a sip of wine. "At least that's the party line."

"That's a terrible answer."

I grin at him for a second before looking back at my wineglass and running my finger around the base so I don't have to make eye contact. "I know. I'm getting there. Dating has been... messy in the past. I have trust issues, at least that's what my very expensive therapist said. Although, I don't think it takes a rocket scientist to figure that out, given my childhood."

I glance up at him and find him focused completely on my face, as if everything I'm saying is utterly captivating. I'm starting to realize that he always watches me like that when I'm talking. When Ben listens, he listens intensely. He holds my eyeline, even when I'm sarcastic or saying things that make most people uncomfortable. He doesn't try to apologize for my past and there's no judgement in his eyes. It makes me want to tell him *everything.*

"It makes it hard for me to connect with people... romantically. Because without trust and emotion, everything felt hollow. Boring, hollow conversations, boring, hollow dates, and boring, hollow sex. At some point I realized it wasn't worth the time because what's the point when I still felt empty at the end of it? So, I focused on work all the time and 'no dating' just became the rule."

It's not a conversation I've ever had with anyone else, not even that crazy expensive therapist. I don't think I've even put this much thought into it before now.

I'm still fiddling with my wine glass when Ben's hand reaches out and brushes his fingertips over the backs of my knuckles. A feathery, glancing touch that is so slight and shockingly intimate. I peek up at him and I swear the air between us charges with electricity when we make eye contact.

There's a tightness around his eyes that gives him a seriousness I've never seen from him before. "This doesn't feel hollow." His voice is low and rough, and it sets desire spreading through my body.

"No," I whisper back. I can't look away from him, but then, I really don't want to. His fingers trace soft little circles on the back of my hand.

"You can trust me," he says.

"No, I can't." My voice comes out too breathy.

Ben grins, his dimples popping even as his eyes bore into me with pure hunger. "Why not?"

"You're too handsome and you're trying to get me to break my only rule. You're obviously trouble." The kind of trouble I'm finding it harder and harder to resist.

Ben circles my wrist with his hand and pulls me out of my chair. I go willingly because I am weak, and I don't want to fight the way he makes me feel. He settles me across his lap and kisses my neck.

"Maybe I'm the best kind of trouble," he says as he runs his lips along the length of my neck.

"I'm inclined to agree with that statement."

Ben chuckles and the sound vibrates through my body, sending up little goosebumps all over my skin. I wrap my arms around his neck and brush my lips against his. He kisses me back softly, one hand supporting my back and the other venturing up my thigh. Every second he spends touching me ratchets up my desire and every tiny movement makes me more and more aware of how wet I am. I'm seriously in danger of needing a new pair of panties, but I couldn't care less at this point.

He deepens the kiss, cradling the back of my neck and dragging my ass across his lap. The feeling of his hard length under me and the moan that rumbles through him is breathtaking, stoking the fire that has been burning in my body all night back into a blaze. I slide my hands under his sweater,

86

seeking out the warmth of his skin. He shivers at my touch and it's insanely gratifying to have that kind of effect on him.

"If you want me to stop," he growls, "now would be a good time to say so." His eyes are dark with lust and the expression matches the aching need swirling inside me.

"Don't stop," I tell him. Ben stands, lifting me like a bride as I pull him close for another scorcher of a kiss. When he slides his tongue into my mouth, I suck on it, making him groan as he walks down the hall towards my bedroom. He sets me on my feet next to the bed, kissing me so deeply it's hard to catch my breath.

Ben breaks the kiss and reaches back to grab his sweater, pulling it off over his head in one smooth motion before tossing it across the room. Reaching out, I undo his belt, unbutton and unzip his pants. He shucks them, leaving his boxers to try to contain the massive erection he's sporting. The sight of his desire and the broad expanse of tanned skin and muscles is enough to make me drool.

"Holy shit, you're beautiful," I whisper. He's all muscles and broad shoulders. I'm suddenly feeling insanely self-conscious but the burning heat in Ben's eyes is licking up and down my body and I don't think he has any complaints at the moment. He reaches for my waist, his eyes dark and hungry as he bites his lip.

"My turn." His voice is low and desperately raspy. His hands slip from my hips down to the hem of my dress. He holds eye contact with me as he bunches the bottom of my dress in both hands and lifts it over my head, just slow enough that I could stop him if I wanted to. I throw my hands up so he can remove it and toss it with his sweater.

I wasn't expecting any of this when I got dressed tonight. I'm wearing a plain black bra and panties. I wish I had picked out better lingerie, but Ben is staring at me like I'm the most beautiful thing he's ever seen. His mouth goes slack as he pulls me towards him. His big hands caress my arm and hip as he draws me in. He kisses me deeply as he dips his fingers into the front of my panties, one large finger sliding between my wet folds eliciting a gasp of pleasure.

I pull him backwards towards the bed and we tumble onto the mattress, a tangle of limbs and bare skin. He tosses his glasses on the nightstand and rolls over on top of me, nudging a thick muscular thigh between both of mine. He's so fucking big and I love the way his body feels pressing over mine, his weight pinning me to the mattress.

I stroke his cock through the thin fabric of his boxers, and he growls low in his throat, yanking my bra down and pulling my nipple into his mouth. The wet heat and scrape of his teeth as he moves back and forth between my nipples sets my aching core into overdrive. If I could just move my hips a little more… but Ben's thigh pins my hips in place while he strokes my skin, holding me captive with his touch.

His hand roams my body, stroking my ribs with his fingertips, cupping my breast, and squeezing my other nipple until I'm a whimpering mess. I slip my hand under the waistband of his boxers to grip his shaft. He's so thick I can't even close my hand around him. I stroke him, enthralled by the feel of his hard length, and he shudders. Ben's hand abandons my breast to grip my wrist and pin it above my head.

"I won't last long if you keep that up, Princess."

I mock scowl at the nickname, even though it's starting to grow on me. Ben grins as he lowers his head to my ribs and gives me a little bite. He slides lower, kissing my stomach and nipping at my hip. My heart races. He leaves a mark on my hip bone before shifting even lower and placing a love bite on my thigh. He hooks his fingers under the waistband of my panties and tugs them down, letting me kick them the rest of the way off before he settles back down between my legs.

I prop myself up on my elbows to watch him because, holy shiitake, is he sexy. His hot breath rolls over my thighs and across my pussy. He locks his eyes on mine as he licks his lips and kisses my mound and I swear to god, nothing has ever felt so intimate. He nuzzles the lips of my pussy with his nose and lips and then I feel Ben lick the entire length of my slit with a wide soft swipe of his tongue.

"Ohmygod," I cry out as my hands fly to the top of his head. I don't know if I'm trying to keep him in place or push him away. He chuckles with his mouth still pressed against me and I shiver with delight. He licks again, letting his tongue delve deeper into my folds as he grips my hips to keep me from squirming. I tunnel my fingers into his soft, wavy hair.

He laps at me over and over, torturing me with long, slow, languid strokes. He circles my clit, pulling it between his lips and sucking gently until I nearly come off of the bed.

"Sweet fucking Jesus," I moan. Never in my life has anything felt as incredible as this. I've always been ambivalent about having someone go down on me. Clearly, I was just doing it with the wrong people.

He doesn't say a word, just growls against my pussy in a self-satisfied way, tonguing me until I'm so desperate to come that my hips are straining against his hands and I'm grinding myself against his hungry mouth.

"Please, I need to come. Please, please, please..." I moan quietly. Ben slides a finger inside me, stroking, and pressing, and twisting as his tongue focuses on my clit. And then another finger stretches me, wiggling and scissoring until he finds the perfect spot on my front wall and strokes his fingers against it.

"Oh God," I whimper. "Yes, Ben, Yes! Please don't stop," My clit is throbbing against his tongue, his movements insistent and firm. Stars explode behind my eyes as my orgasm rips through my body, stronger and hotter than anything I've ever felt. And then I basically lose all cognitive function.

Chapter 21: Ben

Lilah comes like a freight train, my name on her lips while her soaking wet pussy ripples around my fingers. I've never been harder in my life. I watch her face as she comes down, and she looks so blissfully happy. My breath catches in my chest. I want to see that look on her face every day for the rest of my life and know that I'm the one who put it there. I crawl up next to Lilah, scooping her into my arms and cradle her against my chest. She looks up at me with a light in her eyes and an openness that I've never seen in her before.

"Holy hell, Ben. That was... amazing. Better than amazing. I don't know. Words are too hard right now," she says in a dazed, sleepy voice. I laugh quietly and stroke her hair, leaning down to kiss the top of her head. Her leg is thrown over mine, and she's naked except for her displaced bra. Her skin feels like silk against my body.

"Not bad, huh?" I tease her.

She runs a hand over my chest appreciatively. "You definitely do not disappoint."

Her hand wanders lower down my belly. "Although, I can't help but feel you're holding out on me..." Her hand grazes over the waistband of my briefs. I'm about two seconds from begging her to touch me when she slides her hand under the waistband and grips my cock. The feel of her warm hand makes me pulse with need. I turn her face up to mine and kiss her possessively as she strokes me.

"Tell me you want me inside of you," I growl against her lips.

"I want you inside me. I want you so fucking bad," Lilah pants. Her body is trembling in my arms, but her stroking grip on my cock is anything but tentative.

Lilah rolls over and digs a condom out of the bedside table and I stand, dropping my boxers. She looks up at me through her long eyelashes as I take it, rolling it on as slowly as I can in an attempt to not look as insanely desperate as I feel. She watches me and licks her lips, green eyes hungry. Lowering myself over her, I use a knee to spread her legs wider. My dick is nestled against her pussy and she's so wet I can't help sliding myself against her. I cup the back of her neck with one hand, watching her eyes flare with desire as I tease her slick cunt with the head of my dick.

"I know I should be gentle with you, but I don't think I can," I growl in her ear.

"I hate gentle." Lilah presses her feet into the mattress, rolling her soft curves against me. A feral sound rips out of me and I thrust deep inside of her. My brain short circuits as I fill her completely. I can't see, or hear, or even think straight. All I can feel is her tight little pussy stretched around my dick, warm and wet.

"Oh, fuck," she gasps, her nails gripping and biting into my shoulder.

"God, you're so tight," I groan, pressing my forehead to hers. Slowly, I drag myself out of her wet heat and push back in. I thrust harder and faster each time, angling my hips, sinking myself completely and grinding against her clit. She moans and arches again, her pussy clenching around my dick, like hot wet silk. My control evaporates. I pump into her faster and harder while she cries out and rakes her hands through my hair and down my back. Her fingertips grasp at my back as the need builds.

She tests my control with every moan and every touch. I'm at risk of coming embarrassingly fast if she keeps that up. I grab her wrists in one hand and pin them above her head. I nip and suck at her nipples and fuck her hard into the mattress. I reach my free hand between our bodies and press my thumb against her clit, rubbing in time with my strokes.

"Oh god! Ben! Ah!" she cries out.

"Fuck yes, come for me again, Princess," I growl out. Her eyes roll back in her head as another orgasm rolls through her. Her pussy clenches, gripping me like a vise, and it's all I need to fall over the edge with her. I roar as pleasure explodes inside me, and I thrust my release inside of her.

Panting, I roll onto my back, taking Lilah with me and holding on to her with everything I have. Being with her is unlike anything I've ever felt. I feel a surge of unfamiliar possessiveness as she sighs a warm breath across my chest. She is *mine* and I'll do anything to make her happy and keep her by my side.

Eventually, I have to get up to toss the condom and I've never resented a piece of latex so much in my life. She kisses me with a smile as I get back into bed and she takes a turn in the bathroom. I flop on my back on the mattress, deeply content. When she comes back out, she has a nervous look on her face as she approaches me and the bed. I hold my hand out to her. She takes it with a little smile and the worry lines around her eyes ease up. I tug her into bed, her small frame tumbling over mine with a little scream and a laugh.

"Stay," I say, looking into her eyes. I swear my heart is trying to break out of my ribcage to get closer to her.

"Asking or telling?" she replies.

"Telling,"

She laughs and cuddles back against me, resting her head on my chest and sliding an arm over my stomach.

"You know this is my house, right?"

Chapter 22: Lilah

I fall asleep almost immediately, Ben's warm body holding mine. I wake up at 2 am desperately needing to pee and when I come back to bed Ben is half awake. Gently he pulls me back into bed, my back pressed against his very warm, very naked front. I wiggle into place as his arm goes around me and he groans when my butt grinds against him.

Maybe I'm a bit of a tease, but I press back again just to make him groan. His cock throbs against my ass and I can feel it hardening, all in for some playtime, despite the late hour. Ben's lips find my neck, kissing me sweetly as his hand glides up my stomach. His warm hand claims my breast, his fingers tracing circles around my nipple as his kisses turn to little love bites on my shoulder.

"You asleep?" he asks. I can hear the grin in his voice as he nips the sensitive spot where my shoulder meets my neck, making me moan. "I'll take that as a 'no'," he chuckles. His fingers graze over my ribs and belly button, trailing down my thigh. He hooks my knee, pulling it up and over his leg, spreading me wide. His fingers trace the curves of my thigh and hips, making their way to my core. He runs his fingers over my mound and outer lips, but he doesn't push inside. I'm aching for more, desperate to feel his fingers press into me and I moan, making him chuckle.

"See, it's not nice to tease," he whispers as his fingers part my folds, dipping inside, and spreading the moisture around my clit. He rubs lazy circles, content to play with me until I'm simmering, my whole body trembling with need. He moves away, leaning back and I whimper. I was so close! He claims a condom from the nightstand, using his teeth to open it before sliding it on with one hand. He kisses my neck again. "Ready?" he asks in a raspy voice.

I arch my back as he presses the head of his cock to my weeping core, the need overpowering everything else. "Yes," I pant.

With a low groan, Ben pushes into me from behind. He fills me slowly and I feel every nerve singing as he grinds into me. His hand grips my thigh as he strokes in and out at a maddeningly patient pace. The thick head rubs against my G-spot, pleasure spiraling through every thrust until I'm desperate to come, little pleas falling from my lips with each motion.

Ben holds me close, his bottom arm wrapped around my chest, his labored breathing warming my hair. His fingers mercifully pick up their swirling torture around my clit, working me until I'm shaking in his grip.

In an instant, my world implodes, and I cry out his name as the spiraling pleasure overtakes me. He comes a second later, groaning with his face pressed to my shoulder, his body shaking.

I don't know where he gets the energy to get up and take care of the condom, but he manages, and I fall back asleep with his big arm around me.

Waking up is even better. By the time my brain is coming around, I'm already on the verge of orgasm. Ben's head is between my legs and his arms are wrapped around my thighs. I run my hands through his curly hair, and he looks up just long enough to grin devilishly at me and say good morning before diving back in.

"You're spoiling me," I tell him as I lay in bed in a post-orgasmic fog.

"You deserve it," he says, and he smacks the side of my ass. "Come on, breakfast." He jumps up, fully naked and searches the room for his clothes, giving me a breathtaking view of his butt. I watch greedily as he pulls his boxers up. He catches me watching him and beckons me towards him with all the promise of another round in his eyes, but I flop over on my stomach and go limp.

"I'm basically rubber, Ben. You fucked the bones out of me." He laughs and gives me a cocky smile as he pulls up his jeans and slips his glasses back on.

I eye him in the dark frames and I'm suddenly less boneless than I was a minute ago. "Wait! I changed my mind!"

"The glasses?" He asks with amusement. Both of his dimples pop as he grins at me and takes them off, pretending to set them aside. "Should I leave these off so you can control yourself around me?"

I throw a pillow at him and hit him square in the chest.

"Oh, you're going to get it now," he says as he leaps on the bed tickling my ribs. I shriek as I roll over and try to wiggle out from under him, but he straddles my hips and holds both of my hands in one of his, tickling me with the other. I'm cackling, laughing too hard to make a real effort to escape.

"Stop! Please, stop!" I wheeze through shrieks of laughter. "Mercy!" Ben stops tickling me, but he doesn't let me up. Instead, he kisses my ticklish ribs, giving me love bites.

"Can I feed you breakfast yet?" His smile is huge.

"If you must, but if you get clothes, I need clothes too," I tell him as I run my hands through his hair.

"Fine," he sighs. "But for the record, I object."

I throw on some pajama shorts and a tank top and we head to the kitchen. Ben peeks in my fridge, still shirtless, giving me an eyeful of his muscular back and shoulders. I'm hit with a wave of disbelief that this, any of this, is really happening. I can't remember the last time I spent the night with someone, let alone had breakfast together the next morning.

"Where is all of your breakfast food?" Ben asks with a laugh.

"Oh... yeah. I don't really eat breakfast here. I either eat at the bakery or skip breakfast. Sorry," I tell him awkwardly.

"Well, this won't do," he tells me, grinning as he shuts the refrigerator door. He holds his hand out to me. "Come on."

His fingers intertwine with mine as he grabs his sweater and leads me out the front door. We cross my lawn, then his, barefoot and half-dressed. It's insane enough to make a giggle bubble up in my throat, even as the cool spring air pricks little goosebumps all over my bare arms and legs.

Ben tosses his sweater on the back of his couch and parks me at the little dining table in his kitchen with a smiling "Sit."

He starts the coffee maker and pulls an armload of ingredients out of the fridge. The cold air hits my already chilly legs and I shiver, something Ben doesn't miss. It seems he doesn't miss a single thing about me.

"Are you cold?" he asks, eyeing my bare legs with marked interest.

"I'm fine," I say. "I'll warm up in a minute."

Ben gives me a look that says he doesn't believe me. "It's ok to admit you're cold." He swipes his sweater back up and puts it on over my head, kissing me on my hair as I push my arms through the sleeves.

I grudgingly have to admit I already feel better. Normally I'd be salty about being treated like a fragile little flower, but the grin on Ben's face and the look in his eyes makes it obvious that he's enjoying taking care of me.

"Thank you," I tell him.

"Happy to," he replies, and I believe him.

He pours me a cup of coffee and brings it to me with cream and sugar. I add a teaspoon of sugar and dump a ton of half and half into my cup. He watches me and smiles a little half smile before making his cup light on the creamer and a little sugar.

"Are you memorizing how I like my coffee?" I ask him. I cross my legs and lean back, huffing the coffee fumes and loving the way they mix with the smell of Ben's shirt.

"Maybe. How do you like your eggs?"

"Scrambled."

"Bacon or sausage?"

"Do I have to choose?"

"I knew I liked you for a reason." Ben moves easily in the kitchen, happy to cook.

"I've never had a man make me breakfast. Do you do this a lot?" I joke awkwardly. The words just pop out of nowhere. Why did I say that? Why can't I just have one day with Ben where I don't say something stupid?

"Make a woman breakfast? No ma'am. I've never cooked for a woman before. Unless you count my mother or sister." He grins, locking eyes with me until the bacon pops and he has to jump back.

"I'm sorry, I have to ask because I just don't understand. How the hell are you still single?"

Ben's dimple goes so deep that I swear you could use it for a rock-climbing grip.

"That's an easy one. I don't go out much. I dated around a bit, but nothing serious. There was nobody I really wanted before you."

"So you don't go around fingering random women on kitchen counters?" I ask with an arched brow.

Ben chokes on a sip of coffee and coughs, thumping a fist against his chest before answering. "God, no! Just you."

That shouldn't make me as happy as it does, but my chest constricts, my heart thumping, so pleased at being the only one he wants.

If he was anyone else, I'd struggle to believe him. I think about the way he bandaged my head so carefully and the way he consistently puts me first, both in bed and out of it. He's made a real and visible effort to take care of me, and that lights a tiny spark of hope in a part of me that has been dark for a long fucking time. I know I don't trust easily, but for the first time in my life, I truly feel like I can put my faith in someone besides my siblings and my grandmother.

Jesus, this is a lot to process before coffee.

"Where did you get your photos?" I ask him, gesturing at the prints that cover his walls.

Ben grins at one of the photos as he plates our breakfast on two plain white plates. "My sister, Ella, is a photographer. She sends me a print from each assignment. You'll like her. She's a free spirit and much like your grandmother, she has the mouth of a drunken sailor."

Ben puts a plate piled with fluffy scrambled eggs, sausage and crispy bacon in front of me before leaning down to kiss me sweetly.

I may not know where this is going, but I want more of it.

Chapter 23: Ben

We finish breakfast and Lilah insists on helping me with the dishes. Something has shifted between us and it's more than just sex. Lilah opened up a chink in her armor last night and I get the impression that was really big for her. I grew up in a stable home, unless you count *my* antics, so it's hard for me to imagine what it would be like to lose one parent only to be willfully abandoned by the other.

Knowing what I know now, I'm not surprised that trust is a difficult thing for her. I meant it when I said she could trust me. She opened herself up and even if it's just a little crack, I'll keep showing her, day after day, that this is something special.

When we finish putting the dishes away, I don't want to let Lilah go but she insists that she has to get ready for work at the bakery. And since I can't exactly kidnap her and keep her as my sexual hostage, I walk her back home and kiss her at the front door.

"See you tonight," I tell her.

"Are you asking or telling?" she replies.

"Telling," I say with a wink.

"Ok," she says smiling up at me as she stands on her tiptoes to kiss me.

I nearly let her go before noticing something amiss behind her.

"Is the door open?" I ask her.

She turns and presses a hand against the panel, and it swings open freely. I'm positive I heard her shut it behind us when we went to my house this morning, but my mind races with (mostly) rational explanations. An ominous chill creeps up my spine and, even though I know it's probably nothing, I can't let her go inside alone.

I move Lilah behind me and step inside, looking carefully for anything out of the ordinary.

"Wait out here," I say. "I just want to check everything out."

"No way," she says as she follows me inside. "You'll probably just raid my panty drawer."

I can't help myself. I turn and blink at her, completely caught off guard.

I know she's just trying to tease me, but I'm half frustrated at her for making light of a potentially dangerous situation and half in awe of her smart mouth. Her face is pale. She looks scared, but she pushes past me and reaches into the coat closet, producing a wooden baseball bat. She hands it to me and I'm about to thank her before she dives back into the closet, coming out with a metal one. Holy shit, she's awesome.

"Nice," I tell her appreciatively.

She shrugs but gives me a smug little smile as she waves her finger back and forth between the bats. "Asher and Lukas. There's pepper spray in my purse from Julia."

We walk from room to room, looking behind every door, checking every closet, under the bed and even the attic. Infuriatingly, Lilah refuses to stay behind me, ignoring the fact that I have a foot and a half and 120 pounds of muscle on her.

Like everything else about her, I find her stubbornness adorable. I'm pretty sure she'd take a swing at anyone that threatened me right now, and I would straight up love it.

Lilah scoops up a bored looking Frankie as we pass by her cage and when we don't find anything disturbed or any unwelcome visitors, we both relax. Not completely, but enough that Lilah takes the baseball bats and puts them back in the closet. Her brow is still furrowed, and she jumps when she turns the corner and sees me.

"Are you sure you're ok?" I ask her.

"Yeah, fine," she replies. It's the least convincing thing I've ever heard her say.

"I'm going to stay while you get ready."

"You don't have to do that. I'm ok, really."

"I'm staying," I tell her again. She shrugs, but the little lines between her eyebrows smooth out. I'll do anything to make her feel safe and hanging out at her house for half an hour is no hardship. She pulls on my arm, making me bend down so she can kiss me on the cheek before going to shower and get changed. I look at her bookshelves while I kill time. For someone who doesn't do relationships, she sure has a shitload of romance books.

My mom always had a bunch of the old school ones lying around growing up. My sister liked to find the dirty parts and read them aloud to torture me. I don't know how I'd forgotten that. I smile to myself as I run my fingers along some spines with women in fluffy dresses.

Going down a shelf, I pull out a paperback at random and snicker at the cowboy on the cover. He's shirtless, with a Stetson pulled down low, covering his face. I grab another book and there's a shirtless man wearing glasses in front of a library background. "Stud in the Stacks" is scrawled across the cover. Both books are worn in and I flip to a page that has a scrap of paper sticking out like a bookmark.

My eyes nearly bug out of my head. God damn, that's dirty. I read three more pages before replacing the scrap of paper and closing the book with some solid ideas for the future.

Lilah appears to have her books organized by genre, rather than author. There's an entire shelf dedicated to cowboys and another for a bunch of shirtless nerdy guys. I laugh out loud, not because I'm judging but because this is awesome. I fit both stereotypes.

I'm appreciating the clever titles when Lilah comes around the corner. She's showered, changed into light jeans and a red t-shirt and she's towel drying her long hair with a fluffy gray towel. That denim is doing the lord's work, highlighting every curve from her hips down to her calves.

"Sorry, that took a min--" she interrupts herself as she looks at the two books in my hand and makes a choked squeaking sound.

"I think you have a type," I say, laying on my accent extra thick as I hold up the cowboy and hot nerd books up on either side of my face. Now that I

100

know she's got a thing for cowboys, you can sure as shit bet I will use it to my advantage.

"What are you doing?!" she squeaks, racing over to snatch the books out of my hands.

I chuckle and hold them out of reach as I bend down to kiss her.

"I kind of love this about you. These are dirty as hell."

Lilah's cheeks go from pink to scarlet. "Did you read those?" she asks in a strangled voice as she eyes the copy with the makeshift bookmark.

"A little. Just the highlights, really." I watch her face as she tries to recall what the scrap of paper marked, and her eyes go even wider.

"Can I steal this one?" I ask her, holding up the cowboy one. "I might need to bone up."

She groans at the pun and snatches the books from my hands, placing them back on their shelves.

"Stop teasing me. It's not nice." Lilah scowls at me and I see from the crinkle in her forehead, I've hurt her feelings. I wrap her up in a hug, resting my chin on top of her head. She stands still, her arms at her side.

"Hey, don't be upset. I wasn't teasing, Princess. Well, I was teasing a little, but I do want to read it. If you don't want to share, I'll order my own copy."

Lilah sighs and hugs me back. Her arms sliding around my waist is just about the best feeling ever. Just about.

"Fine, but don't start with that one. You have to start at the beginning." She untangles herself and grabs another book off the cowboy shelf. She slaps it into my palm and shakes her head, lips pursed as she gives me a wide-eyed, dubious look.

"I doubt you'll like it."

I kiss her and tuck the book into my back pocket. "We'll see. Just don't tell anyone about this." I give her a wink as we head to the front door. She grabs her purse and phone from the table by the front door, but not before I see an alert on her screen for four missed calls from an unknown number.

The worry I felt when we found her front door cracked creeps back in. I don't want to worry her unnecessarily, but something still feels off. I walk Lilah to her Jeep and kiss her goodbye, trying to hide my concern for the phone calls.

I head back inside my house, and pause just inside the front door, trying to decide what to look at first. Security cameras win out. I check the footage for the time that Lilah was here for breakfast. Unfortunately, the angle is all wrong and I can't see any of Lilah's front walk, much less her driveway or front door. All I can see are cars driving by.

"Fuck," I mutter to myself. I turn my front camera so that it's pointed at her house. I'm torn. I know I should tell her I'm surveilling her house. The problem is, I don't know how to explain the high-tech cameras hidden in my bushes without telling her the truth about what I do. Normal people don't have military grade cameras with motion sensors in their front yard.

I need to figure out the best time to tell her about my extracurricular activities while I'm at it. Shit, I thought this would be easy.

Chapter 24: Lilah

It's been three days since we found my front door open, but I can't seem to shake the feeling that someone is watching me. I can't help but wonder if I'm just being paranoid because my brothers think someone tampered with my Jeep. It's been two weeks and I'm starting to wonder if they overreacted. It wouldn't be the first time they got overprotective.

I skip down the front steps of a French bistro on Main St. I've been cold calling restaurants all over Sonoma, handing out samples of Olive Branch Coffee beans and sales sheets. I've had three calls and two in-person orders and it's only 11 am. I am in a great mood. My phone buzzes and I'm hoping for another order, but the text message I get is even better.

Ben: What do you want for dinner? I'm thinking Pad Thai and a movie at my place.

Ben: P.S. I finished that book and I'm looking for my cowboy boots...

I can't stop the grin that splits my face. Ben gets me. He keeps joking about taking me out on a real date, but I love staying in with him. I've spent every night with him, bouncing back and forth between his house and mine. Lord. If he finds cowboy boots, it's all over for me.

Me: Yes please!

I've been working long hours every day at the bakery. Between helping Olive with classes, prep work, and getting the coffee business cranked up, I'm bone-tired by the end of the day. Spending the evening curled up on the couch with Ben sounds like heaven. I'm so lost in my thoughts I turn the corner without looking and crash into someone.

"Oh, hey Lilah."

Terry. Mother. Fucking. Terry. Of all the people in this town I could bump into, he might be my last choice.

"Excuse me," I say coldly before looking back down at my phone and trying to sidestep him. He doesn't take the hint, choosing to follow me down the street.

"You and your sister are selling coffee now, right?"

I don't respond to Terry's question. I don't work for him anymore and I don't owe him a goddamn thing. I haven't seen him since I left the bar, and I haven't spoken to him since the night I put in my notice. His response at the time was somehow even more disgusting than I had expected. "I'm just glad I won't have to watch you slut it up with the customers anymore." Dickbag.

"If you need to make some sales, I could help you. You should come by the bar one night. We might be able to work something out," he says in what I'm sure he thinks is a smooth voice.

The very thought of working with him again, in any capacity, makes me shudder.

"No thanks," I say before opening the door at my next stop and shutting it in his face. I'm early, but I'd rather browse the little gift shop for 15 minutes than be anywhere near Terry for another 15 seconds.

***

The rest of my day goes by in a blur. A very successful blur. I've got half of the restaurants in town switching over to our coffee, and most of the gift shops are placing orders to carry it. Tomorrow I think I'll drive up and down the valley, hitting all the wineries that have gift shops. I hum happily to myself as I drive back toward the bakery. The weather is amazing, so I take the top off of my Jeep. The wind catches my hair, and I breathe deeply. Sometimes it's good to savor the good.

104

"Shut the fuck up!" Olive squeals when I tell her how well the cold calls went today. "Holy crap. We might need to hire some extra help to handle the packaging and roasting."

My sister is practically vibrating with excitement. We make plans to look at the budget and post a help-wanted ad in the next day or two and then I head out, eager to get home and start my evening with Ben.

I'm halfway home when I hear a rattling coming from the undercarriage of my Jeep.

"Jesus, what now?" I mutter. I swear, I'm one car problem away from selling this thing and buying the ugliest, most practical thing I can find. I pull over, hoping it's just a piece of loose trim or a stick stuck under the bumper. In other words, something I could take care of myself.

Using the flashlight on my phone, I kneel and peer under the back side of the car. Nothing looks amiss... just a bunch of metal. I'm about to stand up when I swear, I see a blinking red light coming from behind the back wheel.

It's a bomb! My lizard brain shrieks. Except, when I take a better look at it, it's coming from a tiny black rectangle of plastic. In my admittedly very limited knowledge of bombs, that doesn't look like it could explode a Barbie Jeep, let alone damage my full-size one.

Gingerly reaching around the tire, I touch the rectangle with my fingertips. It pivots and makes a little rattle. Well, at least that's the sound identified. I grab it, trying to see if I just need to click something back, but it breaks off in my hand. No. Not breaks. It pries off like a magnet.

I frown as I look at it, turning it over in my palm. It's devoid of markings, just a tiny, dull, blinking light. It's covered in mud splatters and looks worn. The backside has one powerful magnet and a spot where another must have been glued on. I guess that's why it was rattling. I just don't understand why it would be attached with magnets and not wired in.

Cars are flying by and I don't want to hang out on the side of the road, so I hop back into the driver's seat and toss the part over to the passenger side, making a mental note to message Asher and Lukas about it when I get home.

105

I pull into the driveway almost an hour earlier than usual and holy mother of god. The view is so good. My heart skips a beat at the sight of Ben, shirtless and glistening with sweat, pushing his lawn mower through my overgrown grass. He grins at me and my heart doesn't just skip. It sprints and trips, tumbling through my chest and rattling my ribs.

"Thank you, Jesus," I whisper to myself. He cuts the engine just as I hop out. I flip my sunglasses up on top of my head and whistle at him as he stalks over to me.

"You're early! This was supposed to be a surprise," he says before giving me a big sweaty hug and picking me up off my feet.

"Ew!" I laugh as I squirm in his arms. I don't really mind sweaty Ben. Given the right situation, it's hot as hell. Ben sets me back on my feet and cups my face as he kisses me. He smells like sweat, freshly cut grass, and gasoline.

"This shouldn't be doing it for me, but it definitely is," I tell him, running a finger over his sweaty chest.

"Glad to hear it." Ben can't contain his smug smile. "I know we said takeout tonight, but I have a better idea," he says.

"Oh, really?"

"Yeah, I'm going to finish up and shower. We've got a reservation at 7." A little thrill runs through me because god do I love it when he takes charge. The feminist in me is still trying to come to grips with it, but my inner sex kitten is all in.

"All right. I'll go get cleaned up," I say in a flirty voice. I smile to myself because I know exactly what I'm going to wear.

I shower and shave my legs, blow-dry my hair and put on a little makeup before digging in my closet for the dress that Sally gave me. It's impossible not to smirk as I lay it on the bed. As much as Ben appreciated it the first time around, he will lose his shit when he sees me in it with a decent bra and my hair done.

I'm ready by 6:30 and just slipping my shoes on when I hear a knock on

106

the door. I peek through the front window to make sure it's Ben before opening the door.

Did I think he was sexy when he was dirty and shirtless? Because now he's all cleaned up in cream-colored chinos and a navy-blue linen dress shirt with the sleeves rolled up, and my tongue is practically on the floor. I never really got the whole "arm porn" thing until right this second. I think I'm officially converting to the Church of Muscular Forearms.

His normally unruly hair is tamed and styled, making him look even more handsome than usual. The icing on the cake is the intense, hungry way he's watching me from behind his glasses. He's like every hot nerd fantasy I've ever had, all rolled into one.

He looks me up and down, lust painted in his every feature. "You look good enough to eat, Lilah." His voice has that husky, I'm-about-to-give-it-to-you quality it gets when he's turned on, and at this point he's basically conditioned me to ruin panties when I hear it.

It's all I can do to keep from moaning out loud.

"We can just stay in," I tell him, pointing my thumb over my shoulder at the couch. Two nights ago, he had me sprawled out in that exact spot while he ate me out. I would be so, so down for a repeat performance. I lick my lips and adjust the neckline of my dress, trying to coax Ben inside.

Ben gives me a dark, hungry look, a muscle ticking in his jaw as he steps over the threshold. He uses his massive frame to crowd me back against the wall so he has room to shut the front door.

"If I didn't know any better, I'd say you're trying to tempt me to miss our reservation..." his deep, controlled voice sends a shiver right through me and moisture soaking my panties.

"Maybe I am," I say with a shallow breath.

His lips pull up in a smirk. "Naughty girl." He runs a finger under the neckline of my dress, following the dips of my breasts, making goosebumps rise across my entire body. He slides a hand behind my neck, holding me in place as he kisses me hard enough to make my lips tingle. He slips his free hand under my dress and strokes my white satin panties, growling and

107

pressing a finger against the wet fabric to stroke my clit. My gasp is swallowed by his lips as he rubs gentle circles. Ben rests his forehead against mine, lips parted as he watches me melt under his touch.

"Yes," I moan. "Please, yes..."

And then the bastard takes his finger away and, casual as can be, checks the time on his watch.

"What the--?"

"Don't want to be late, Princess," he says with a self-satisfied smirk as he reaches back and opens the front door, gesturing for me to precede him.

"You suck," I say indignantly. He chuckles, his dimples on full display.

He leans in to whisper in my ear, "You started the teasing but I promise I'll make it up to you later."

I'm tempted to whine about it, but decide it'll be more fun to make it hard on him to hold out. Pun intended. I smooth an imaginary wrinkle on his shirt collar, putting a sweet, innocent look on my face while running my fingernails over his chest.

"That's ok. I can wait. I got myself off in the shower anyway," I tell him, patting his arm and kissing him on the cheek. "Twice," I say before swishing out the front door, leaving him to cope with that mental image.

Chapter 25: Ben

Fuck. Me. Running.

I bite my fist as she sashays her way to my car, swinging her ass just for me. God, this is going to be so much fun.

Lilah tells me about her day on the way to the restaurant. She fills me in on each of the shops and restaurants that have already ordered coffee from her. There's a pause in the conversation as she looks out the window. "Thanks for mowing my lawn. You didn't have to do that."

"I figured I owe you. For all the times I woke you up and, you know, the head wound."

Lilah laughs, and the sound is like music. I love it. In that moment, as crazy as it sounds, I realize that I'm falling in love with her. "Besides, I know you don't have a mower yet. Being a new homeowner and all."

She grimaces, "I know I really need to get one. Would you believe that it never occurred to me that I would need one?"

I laugh. "Yeah, I could see that, but I don't think you should buy one. It's a waste of money when you can just let me take care of it for you."

"I feel like I'm taking advantage of you..." she trails off. "But maybe I could trade you something. How do you feel about cookies?"

I put a hand over my heart. "If you make me homemade cookies, I'll never let you go."

"Deal," she blushes. Cookies are a bonus, but I wonder if she realizes how much she's let her guard down with me. I've chipped through layers of stubborn independence, and I feel like she's finally letting me in. I have a moment of cold guilt when I think about the things I haven't confessed.

I work when she works and because she has no point of reference on how long my legitimate security work takes, she's never questioned what I do with the extra time. I told her all about the corporate hack I did on a major bank, and the weak spots I found that could have been used to leak customer info. She listened, mouth agape when I told her that my last phishing email test came back with 38% of the users not just opening them, but giving out personal information. It was enough to make me reach for a beer at three in the afternoon.

What I didn't tell her is that I also helped a woman and her child start a fresh life in Canada and anonymously reported their abuser to the Justice Department, handing over the entire contents of his hard drive and cloud storage. He may have also accidentally emailed all of his personal and professional contacts an audio file ranting about some of his favorite racist topics.

I realize that I have an overactive sense of justice, but I just can't let people like that go about their lives. It eats at me. It's not like I'm planting anything on them or creating something to use against them. It's all right there in their digital files. Every filthy, awful, incriminating thing that they think no one will ever see because they put a weak ass password on it.

It's starting to feel like I'm not much better, hiding so much of what I do from Lilah. Even knowing that what I'm doing is morally right, my methods might be ethically flawed. It's very much a gray area, and I've spent enough time with Lilah to know she often sees things a little more black and white. I can't hide this forever. I just have to put my faith in her affection for me.

I pull into a parking spot, resolving to come clean tomorrow because the last thing I want to do is ruin our first actual date. Weaving our fingers together, I lead Lilah inside. The hostess smiles brightly at us when I give her my name. Lilah leans her shoulder into me while the hostess collects our menus and I take advantage of the delay to kiss the top of her head, closing my eyes and inhaling the smell of her shampoo.

"This way," the hostess singsongs. I place my hand on Lilah's lower back just to touch her as much as possible. We follow the hostess through the restaurant to the small back patio.

"This is beautiful, Ben," she sighs. Little lights are hanging from giant oak trees, and a small fountain separates our table from the rest of the patio. I glance down at her and my chest constricts as she gives me an adoring look, her eyes bright and filled with joy. That look, that smile, is everything I need.

110

She is everything that is good and honest and joyful. When I'm with her, I'm reminded that the world isn't such a dark and terrible place.

I hold her chair out for her and sit in the one next to her, but she's still too far away. Hooking my foot through the leg of her chair, I pull her closer. She makes a tiny squeaking sound as if surprised but rests her warm little hand on my thigh, clearly not averse to the closeness.

Lilah picks up her menu in her right hand, her left still on my thigh. Her fingers stroke little absentminded circles as she decides what to order. At least I'm assuming it's absentminded. That or she's intentionally trying to torture me. The little smirk playing on her lips as she reads the menu would suggest the latter. Thank god there's a tablecloth to hide my rapidly thickening problem.

I lean back and throw an arm around her shoulder, spreading my legs and letting her have free rein of my thigh. I have no shame when it comes to my attraction for her. If she's determined to turn me on, who am I to argue?

"What are you in the mood for?" I ask, throwing a pointed look at the front of her dress, letting her know exactly what I'm looking forward to. She blushes, pausing her petting fingers as a very bored looking waiter approaches. He gives us a rundown on the specials, all the while looking like he could not give less of a fuck.

He takes our drink order and Lilah orders the braised short ribs. I go with the steak, and hand our menus back. As soon as the waiter leaves, Lilah starts her teasing little fingers back up, moving ever closer to the tent in my pants of her own making. This feels like a game of chicken, but it's one that I have no intention of losing.

The waiter brings our wine, setting it in front of us, promising that our food will be right out.

I lean over to whisper in her ear. "I love it when you touch me like that but now all I can think about is how good you taste. How I want to spread you out on this table and lick your pussy until you can't see straight. I want to bend you over and fuck you so hard you forget your own name." She shivers and licks her lips, squirming in her seat.

"You're not going to be able to hold still now, are you?" I ask. "I bet I could slip a finger under your panties and you'd be soaking wet for me." Lilah moans softly, so quiet I can barely hear it, but I feel it seep through every inch of my body.

Suddenly I cannot wait any longer.

"Bathroom. Now," I tell her. She gives me a wide-eyed look but doesn't hesitate to throw her napkin on the table and stand up, walking through the back door of the restaurant. Through the window, I watch her pass through one of the bathroom doors. There's no patience left in my body as I stand and follow.

I hope that our waiter is as inattentive for the next five minutes as he looked.

I walk as casually as I can, but if anyone is watching, I doubt they'd miss the hard-on I'm sporting. I open the bathroom door, close it behind me, and lock it. Lilah is leaning against the far wall, her eyes burning with anticipation. I don't waste a second unbuckling my belt and unzipping my pants. I've got my dick in hand and stroke it as she watches, licking her parted lips. She wordlessly holds up a condom between two fingers.

I take it, sheathing myself as quickly as I can. Her breathing is fast and shallow, making her tits heave at the front of her dress.

"Turn around," I demand gruffly. She faces the wall and places her palms on it, bending forward slowly, making her dress hitch up, inch by tantalizing fucking inch. She watches me while I sink to my knees behind her. I toss the bottom of her dress up her back, out of my way, and strip her soaking wet panties to her ankles.

She gasps as I press a finger into her core and immediately add a second. She's so hot and slick that my mind goes blank. I can't think about a single thing beyond the need wracking my body. Grabbing her hips, I bury my face in her pussy, focusing all of my energy on the area around her clit. She tastes so fucking good, tangy with musky desire. I pick up speed, practically assaulting her clit until she's shaking and whimpering and so fucking needy that I can't wait anymore.

112

My cock is aching. Throbbing with need. I stand, and in one rough thrust, sink deep in her pussy. Lilah lets out a low moan, her eyes glazed as she watches me over her shoulder.

"Yes. Oh, god. Yes. Please," she whispers.

I wrap my forearm around the front of her shoulders, pulling her back into me as I pet her clit with the other hand. She feels so fucking good.

She's trembling, her body like bowstring, ready to snap. I cover her mouth and whisper in her ear, "You like that cock, don't you?"

She moans against my hand, her pussy gripping me like a hot fist. I'm desperate to come, but I won't do it until I make her lose control. "I need to feel you come. Be a good girl and come on my dick. I need to feel that tight little pussy strangle my cock."

Lilah's so wet, I can feel her juice on my balls as she comes, cunt clamping down on me like a fucking vise as she screams against my hand. I come hard with a grunt, muffled in her hair. We sag against the wall, catching our breath, but there's no time to hold her like I want to.

Stripping the condom, I tie it off and wrap it in a paper towel before tossing it in the trash. Lilah hurriedly wets a paper towel, handing it to me with a blissful grin. We clean up quickly, aware that our waiter might be missing us by now. Lilah is holding her panties and looking like she's not sure what to do with them.

"They touched the floor," she says, looking truly grossed out. I snatch them and tuck them into my pocket.

Without a word, I kiss her and duck out of the door. I make it back to the table without seeing a single person. Lilah rejoins me a minute later, looking very smug as she takes a sip from her wine glass. Just as she sets her glass back on the table, the waiter arrives with our food.

"Sorry about the wait, folks," he says dully. "Kitchen got a little backed up. Dessert is on the house tonight." He's gone before either of us can respond.

"I already had dessert," I say under my breath, and Lilah giggles.

Chapter 26: Lilah

I cannot believe I just did that. Scratch that. I cannot believe we *got away* with that.

"I've never had sex in public before," I whisper to Ben once the waiter leaves us alone. He gives me a huge, dimpled grin.

"Me either. But I'm game any time you are."

I don't know how all of this will play out, but I'll be fantasizing about the way my hands hit the bathroom wall as I bent over for him when I'm 80. The rush I felt when he walked into the bathroom and locked the door, eying me with a predatory focus. I try to contain the blush rising in my cheeks as I think about it, but it's a losing battle.

With my need for Ben satisfied, at least temporarily, we share a quiet dinner. We pick a trail to hike and a winery to visit on Saturday before family dinner at Gran's. Ben fills me in on his sister's latest assignment in Nova Scotia and her relief at leaving D.C. behind.

Every now and then, I catch him putting his hand in his pocket. The one where he stashed my wet panties. He smirks a little and the thought of him rubbing them and thinking about me makes me wet all over again. Did I say I was satisfied? I lied.

We finish our complimentary dessert and I almost feel guilty about it. It's not like we were waiting miserably for our food. The waiter brings the check and Ben snaps it up before I can even reach for it.

"You should let me pay for it!" I try to take the bill, but Ben holds it out of reach. "You keep paying for everything."

Ben drops his chin, giving me a *just-try-it* face. "I could never live it down if my mother found out I let you pay for our first date. She'd have her entire church congregation shaming me for years."

I open my mouth to argue, but then I realize this *is* our first date. How did I miss that?! "I can't believe you tricked me into going on a date without having to actually ask me," I say. Ben grins at me, looking very proud of himself.

"You're sneaky as hell," I mutter. He might be sneaky but I'm not mad at it. "You're lucky this is the single greatest date I've ever been on," I tell him, pursing my lips. Ben reaches over and pulls me into his lap, threading his hands through the hair at the back of my head and kissing me deeply. It's long and slow and I can still taste the chocolate cake we shared. He kisses me like we have all the time in the world.

He smiles against my lips. "Me too."

***

I'm brushing my teeth in Ben's bathroom when I remember I was supposed to ask my brothers about that broken part on my Jeep. I blame Ben. He distracted me with dinner and sex, and now it's gotten way too late to call one of them. Well, Lukas might be up, but I don't want to take the chance of interrupting him if he's "entertaining" a woman. I shudder as I spit the toothpaste out in the sink and rinse. First thing tomorrow, I'll deal with it, I promise myself.

Ben steals in behind me as I straighten up and watches me as I wipe a tiny fleck of toothpaste from the corner of my mouth. He pulls my hair to the side, placing a little kiss at the juncture of my neck and shoulder. His eyes hold mine and there's something so powerful in the way he watches me.

Our rendezvous in the bathroom might have taken the edge off for a while, but judging from the look in Ben's eyes, it certainly hasn't kept him satisfied for long. I watch his face in the mirror as he slides his hands around my waist.

"How do you do that?" I ask quietly.

"Do what?" he asks, nuzzling the shell of my ear with his nose.

"When you look at me like that... you make me feel like you really see me."

115

Ben smiles against my neck. "That's because I do see you. You're strong and beautiful. You are kind but don't let people walk all over you. You don't hold back or make yourself less just to appease anyone else. I see every inch of you."

I let out the ragged breath I've been holding in. I've never heard someone describe me like that, and holy shit, is it a turn on.

His big warm palms move over the fabric of my dress and spread over my belly, pulling me back into his firm body. He kisses my neck again and growls in approval when I rub my ass against him.

The adorable, smiling Ben that everyone else sees is giving way to the dirty-talking, possessive man that only I get to see and I fucking love it. No one would look at him and know how dark his eyes get when he tosses his glasses on the counter and reaches down the front of my dress to cup my breast. He bites my neck gently and teases the peak of my nipple. Every movement is slow and powerful, a complete turnaround from the frantic sex at the restaurant. He's controlling the pace and I'm perfectly happy to follow his lead.

His hand slips under my dress, petting my thigh and bare hip. I think about my panties, still in his pocket, and moan quietly.

"What do you want, Lilah?" he rasps.

I pause, unsure how to word this but after a beat I just spit it out. "I like it when you're in charge." I've already given him way more control sexually than I ever would have with someone else, and the more I let him take control, the more I like it. "I liked it when you told me what to do."

He nips my neck and watches me as one side of his mouth pulls up in the crooked smile I love so much. "Take your dress off." His voice is gravelly and sends a thrill running through me. I lick my lips, holding his gaze as I unzip the side zipper and lift my dress over my head.

Ben's eyes are dark with desire, "God, you are so beautiful," he murmurs next to my ear. He unhooks my bra, slowly sliding the straps down my arms and letting it fall to the floor in front of us. I'm spellbound watching our reflections. His eyes devour me as he slides a hand up to cup my breast,

116

pinching my nipple and the sight of his masculine hands on my body is so erotic that my core clenches with need.

He winds his fingers in my hair and pulls my head back to look straight into his eyes. I'm wet beyond all reason. I can feel the heat of my arousal as it drips down my thighs and I am painfully aware of how empty my pussy is. I try to shift my weight, squeezing my thighs together to ease the ache, but it just makes my ass rub against the enormous erection straining the zipper of Ben's pants.

"Go lay on the bed," he says. His voice is quiet, laced with confidence and growling need. Sweet Jesus, I'm so turned on that my knees tremble as I cross to the bed. I do what he says, laying in the middle of the bed, naked and practically panting with excitement. He follows me and stands at the foot of the bed, watching and thinking. The streetlights filtering through the window cast just enough light to see the appreciation in his eyes.

Ben rolls his shirt sleeves up once more on each side, the muscles in his forearms flexing. I seriously wonder if I might get off just watching him adjust his cuffs.

"Touch yourself," he growls.

"What?!" I ask. Oh, I definitely heard him right, but that really wasn't what I expected.

"You heard me," he chuckles. "Show me what you do when you think about me."

Jesus Christ, my heart is hammering inside my chest. "That's..." What? I *asked* him to take control. I *asked* him to tell me what to do. I just need to grow a pair, metaphorically.

I try to control my racing pulse as I close my eyes and trail my fingertips over my ribs. I imagine Ben's hand cupping my breast, his mouth on my nipple, his hot breath across my skin, and the way he nips at my ribs as he moves down my body. Ben moans and I open my eyes. He's unzipped his pants, and he's holding his cock, sliding his hand up the length of it. Even in the dim light, I can see how hard and swollen it is. Moisture beads at the tip as he strokes himself, rolling the head in his fist.

I'm frozen, mouth hanging open as I stare, completely mesmerized at the sight of him. I've never watched a man jerk off before. Those muscles I love so much bunch in his forearm as he rotates his grip.

"Show me how wet you are." His voice is a rumbling command. My nerves have evaporated. All that's left is my desire to please him. Using two fingers, I part the lips of my pussy, showing him exactly what he wants to see before slipping them inside with a moan. I've never been this wet in my life.

"Fuck," Ben groans. "Tell me what you think about when you finger yourself."

"You," I whimper. "Your mouth on me. Your big fingers in my pussy. Mine are too small. They don't feel as good as yours," I sigh as I pump in and out.

Ben lets out a feral sound as he kneels on the bed, gripping my wrist and bringing it to his mouth. He sucks the honey off my fingers with a moan and puts them back inside me.

"Don't stop," he commands. I do as I'm told, fingering myself while he watches. The muscle in his jaw ticks as his stormy eyes flick between my face and my pussy, so slippery that my fingers are making obscenely wet sounds as I touch myself for him. I could come but I know it won't be as good as when he does it. My fingers just aren't long enough or thick enough to fill me the way I like it.

"Ben- Ben, please..." I'm so turned on I can barely keep it together, let alone form complete sentences. "I need more."

He stands, retrieving a condom from the nightstand and rolls it up slowly before climbing over me. He pulls my fingers from my pussy and pins my hands over my head.

"Oh my god, yes," I moan as Ben uses his knee to spread my legs. He presses the fat head of his cock to my entrance and sinks into me, slowly stretching me around him until he's buried in me. He rocks in and out of me, so slowly I think he might be trying to kill me, until I'm pleading for more, faster, harder.

118

He drags my legs up, hooking my knees around his elbows and drills into me like precision machinery, stroking me higher and tighter as he praises me.

"God, I love your tight little pussy. You feel so fucking good," he breathes against my neck. "So good. You're going to come for me. I want to feel it. Come on my dick. Now."

My orgasm spirals up as Ben strokes deeper, sweeping me along in what feels like endless pleasure. It keeps building and rolling through me as his body shakes. With one last brutal thrust, he comes inside me.

There's a loud crack and the bed lurches sideways, sending us rolling off the edge. Somehow, I land underneath him, caged in by his arms. The back of my head is cradled in one of his enormous hands, protecting me from cracking it on the floor, even as his cock is still buried balls deep inside me. We stare at each other in shock for a second as we simultaneously come to the same conclusion and start laughing.

"We broke the bed," I cackle. My laughter makes my internal muscles contract, squeezing his now overly sensitive dick. Ben scrambles off of me in self-defense and falls to the floor next to me, laughing hysterically.

Chapter 27: Ben

Once we pull ourselves together, we shift the mattress to the floor and look at the bed frame. One of the wooden joints cracked and splintered. I don't need to be a woodworker to know that sucker is completely unfixable.

"I guess we get to go bed shopping tomorrow. You can help me test out the new candidates," I say with a suggestive smile. "Do you want to go back to your house?" I honestly don't care where I sleep as long as I'm with her while I do it.

"Nah, I don't feel like getting dressed," she says. She makes a valid point, I think as I look her up and down. Keeping her naked is definitely the better plan. We pile all the pillows and blankets I have in the house on top of the mattress and make a nest. I lay down, pulling her close. Her soft curves press against me and she throws a leg over my thigh. I drift off to sleep happier and more relaxed than I've ever felt.

I wake up in the middle of the night to a strange buzzing sound. Bees? Lilah is still curled up next to me, seemingly untroubled by it, but my sleep-addled brain can't rest until I find the source.

I wake up enough to realize the sound is definitely not bees. It sounds electronic. Following the sound with my eyes, I see Lilah's purse on the floor across the room and a light shining out of it. The grogginess clears but I'm dead tired so when the buzzing stops, I close my eyes, drifting off again. I don't think more than a minute goes by before the vibrating starts back up. Worried that it could be important, I gingerly pull my arm out from under Lilah's head and stand. Grabbing her phone, I slip out of the room before looking at the caller ID.

Unknown Number.

I'm getting really sick of these people calling her phone all the time. 1:56 am. Who the fuck is making spam and telemarketing calls at this time of night? The right thing to do is ignore it and go back to bed, but I'm tired and honestly kind of pissed off. So, I don't do the right thing. I swipe to answer the call, saying nothing.

120

Nobody answers, and I'm annoyed. I expected a robo-caller at the very least.

I hang up and turn to head back to bed, but the phone rings before I can take two steps. I answer it silently again, wishing I had just powered the damn thing down. There's nothing on the other end for endless seconds. It must be an auto-dialer that's not connected to a message or something. Whatever is going on, I can hack the phone company in the morning and figure this out before I finish my coffee.

I'm about to hang up when I hear someone breathe on the other end. My blood runs cold and I silently pray my brain is playing tricks on me. Scrunching my face up, I try to focus and pick up the soft sounds in the background. There's a slight hum and another, heavier breath.

"Hello?" I ask. My voice sounds gruff. Good, I think as there's movement on the other end of the line, a bumping sound and a male grunt.

I hold the phone out and look at it with disgust. Rage fills my senses, clouding my vision as I squeeze the phone in my fist. I am so angry my hands are shaking. I kind of wish I could punch something right now.

Placing the phone back to my ear, I growl in my most menacing voice. "Listen here, fucker. Stop calling this number or I'll rip your balls off and shove them so far up your ass you'll be tasting them for weeks."

After ending the call, I stare at the phone, willing whoever that was to call again just so I can follow through on my threat. But the phone stays dark for the next several minutes while I stand there glaring at it.

She's been getting these calls almost daily since we started seeing each other. I can't be sure, but I don't think there's been even one night where she didn't get at least one call from an unknown number. But she's never answered one in front of me.

I wonder if she knows... The more I think about it, I'm sure she doesn't. There's no way she could just ignore it and play it off so casually. Surely she would at least be rattled when the calls came through. But she just rolls her eyes and silences them, carrying on like nothing happened.

I want to wake her up. I want to talk to her *right now* but when I walk back into the bedroom and see her, I can't do it. Her hair is fanned over the pillow and she's sprawled out across the whole bed. Arms and legs everywhere and a soft smile tugging at her lips. She's still naked and only half covered by the blanket. She looks so peaceful. Waking her up won't solve anything. This can wait until the morning.

I shut her phone down and set it back in her bag before settling back on the mattress with her. I have to move her arms and legs to make enough room, but I'm rewarded when she sleepily nuzzles into my side.

"Love you..." she sighs, still mostly asleep.

I freeze, my heart pounding out *YES-YES-YES* in my chest. I don't move, praying that if I hold still enough, maybe she'll say it again.

But she doesn't. Lilah has gone boneless against me again, and the only sound is her quiet breathing. I exhale, holding her tighter to me as I press a kiss to the top of her head.

I don't know how long I lay awake like that. I breathe in her scent and try to relax, but the phone call spirals in my brain along with a list of things I need to do in the morning. Hack her phone provider, find out who has been making those calls, dig a shallow grave somewhere remote.

Not really. I can take someone down without laying a finger on them, but I suddenly get why men get violent and territorial over their women. The thought of anyone harassing or harming a single hair on Lilah's head makes my blood turn to lava.

Chapter 28: Lilah

I sleep soundly through the night. I always sleep well when I'm with Ben. I've been blaming it on the oxytocin coma he induces with countless orgasms, but when I wake up warm and cozy, tucked into his side, I can't help but think it's more than that. He's become my happy place.

I haven't had a happy place since I lost my mom and in a lot of ways, I think my last true home died with her.

My grandma loved us and took care of us when our dad left, but I don't think I ever felt completely at home, even with her. In the back of my head, there was always this nagging fear that my dad would come back and make us live with him again. That I would lose the safety and stability Gran provided.

After countless college dorms and shared apartments, I thought buying my own house would give me that home feeling. Nothing feels like home except for Ben, and I'll take a mattress on the floor any day if it means I get to be with him. He's almost too good to be true, and I have to consciously suppress the gnawing fear that I'll lose him.

I rub my chest and breathe; I'm falling for him. Shit, I'm not falling. I've *fallen* and I don't even know when it happened. I'm in love with him and it's not like I thought it would be. There was no bungee-cord-tied-to-a-bridge-JUMP moment. There was no leap of faith or grand gesture.

No. There are a million cocky, dimpled grins. There's a mountain of all the little, thoughtful things Ben does for me. Nights spent sleeping in the same bed and the feeling of his arms around me, his breath whispering over my hair.

Every moment adds up to this feeling in my chest, the dual sensation of my ribs squeezing the life out of me and my heart exploding with joy. This is the home I've been missing. It's not a house, or a place; it's just him.

Ben is completely passed out next to me, head thrown back and snoring softly. He's so adorable. I want to run my fingers through his hair and play with his curls. I have a crazy moment where I wonder if our kids would get his hair. I'd like that. Crazy, right?

I should let him sleep; I decide. If I knock out the work I need to do this morning, I can spend the rest of the day with him.

I carefully wiggle my way to freedom and find my clothes. I just need to run home and grab my laptop. I'll pop right back over, sit in his living room, get some work done, and then we can make breakfast together.

Pleased with my plan, I grab my purse and slip out his front door. I scoot across the yard and unlock my door. My house is so empty and silent. An unpleasant feeling creeps up my spine. Something feels off but I shrug it off, chalking it up to missing Ben and wanting to get back to him.

I change out of my dress, throwing on a pair of skinny jeans with a tank top and a slouchy sweater. Ben's house is basically an ice castle. I have to layer up if I'll be at his house for any length of time, not that I mind an excuse to wear my fall sweaters year-round.

I check on Frankie, make sure she has plenty of water and give her some fresh food. She doesn't require much, but I still feel guilty leaving her here while I spend the day with Ben. He's got a soft spot for her, and I bet he'd set up an extra space for her at his house if I mention it.

I pull her ball out of the corner so she can roll it around and watch her for a minute as she bops it. I grab my laptop bag from its hook by the front door and head back out, locking the door behind me.

I cross back towards Ben's house, but something catches my eye. His Jaguar looks wrong, and it takes me a second to see he has a flat. No, I realize as I get closer. He has four flat tires. Holy shit. I circle the car, frowning. The deflated rubber looks like it's pooling under the weight of his car, but that's not all. Someone keyed every single panel of Ben's car. There are long ugly gouges in the paint with shorter, diagonal and zigzag marks that look like someone was slashing it with some serious aggression.

Great. So much for our relaxing morning. I'm heading back inside to wake Ben up when I hear his front door fly open and he steps out, looking panicked. My heart stutters at the worry on his face and the way his relief at seeing me washes it away.

"I woke up, and you were missing," he says as he joins me on the front porch. He pulls me in, holding me tight and planting a kiss on top of my head. I'd smile at the exasperation in his voice, but I'm more worried about the damage to his car at the moment. He loves that thing.

"Ben, your car..." I glance back at his car, a sick feeling in my stomach as his eyes shift from me to the ruined rubber and carnage. I follow him, rubbing his back and watch as his face shifts from confusion to fear so fast it's startling.

"Lilah, get inside," he says.

"What? Why?"

"Because someone slashed my goddamn tires."

"Well, yeah. I mean, that's pretty obvious,"

Ben pulls me towards the front door. "Please, just come inside," he pleads, half dragging me.

I pull back a little. He's being ridiculous. "It's not like it's going to explode or anything. It was probably just some teenagers being shitty."

"Look at the hood, Lilah." His voice sounds like he's being tortured. From this angle, I realize the scratches on the hood aren't random like the sides. The words "Stay away from her" are carved into the black paint in ugly, jagged strokes. It's barely legible, even looking at it head-on.

"Why would someone do that to you?" I whisper. Even as I say it, I feel like my body is being dunked in a tank of ice water.

He doesn't meet my eyes when he answers. "I can think of a couple reasons. Some might be my own fault, but... Jesus." He rubs his hand down his face. "Look, I've been meaning to tell you some stuff. Can you please just come inside?" Ice water, nothing. I'm treading water in the Arctic Circle.

I let him lead me inside, but there's panic bubbling up in my throat, choking me.

125

"Ben," I try to swallow. "What aren't you telling me?"

He closes the door behind us, locking it, before he scrubs his hands over his face with both hands. "I promise, I'll tell you everything, but you have to listen. You have to know that I'm going to fix it."

"Fix it? Fix what?" That hysterical edge in my voice? Yeah, I totally can't help it.

Ben takes my laptop bag and purse off my shoulder and sets them on the counter, pulling everything out of them. I'm frozen in place, wondering what the hell he thinks he's doing until he grabs the bottom of both bags, holding them upside down and shaking them out. A pencil, a tampon, two lipsticks and a couple paper clips skitter across the counter before hitting the floor.

"What the fu-"

"SHH!" He says sharply.

I'm so angry I'm shaking. "Don't shush m- Hey!" I exclaim as he pops the battery out of my laptop. He picks up my phone, making sure it's turned off. I watch, mouth agape, as he takes my laptop and phone and shoves them both in his fridge.

"What are you doing?!" I yell.

Ben holds his hands up, his voice placating. "Relax, I'll make sure they're clean in a minute, but until I know what we're dealing with, that's the safest place for them. It's reasonably soundproof and should block any signals."

"Oh... Okaaay. Are we talking about the CIA, little green men?" I ask. He's lost his damn mind. I briefly wonder if he's pretty enough to stay with, even if he's low-key totally nuts. No. Probably not. Right? I mean… maybe.

But then he turns back to me, rolling his chocolate brown eyes. "Don't be sarcastic, Princess."

My heart and my head are at war, but he's earned a little trust, right? "Start talking, Ben."

Chapter 29: Ben

My mind races as I lick my lips and try to decide where to start. This went from being a minor confession to a tangled shit-heap of secrets in just a couple of hours. Lilah looks like she's debating the best way to get me committed to a mental facility. To be fair, I probably looked a little crazy when I shoved her laptop and phone between the milk and a bottle of ketchup.

"I know from experience how easy it is to use a phone or laptop as a listening device or to log keystrokes. They both need to be bricked until I can go through them and make sure there's no malware."

"What are you talking about?" Lilah laughs, a hysterical edge creeping into her voice.

"The phone calls. The ones from unknown numbers. Did you ever answer them?" I ask her.

Lilah looks exasperated, her green eyes flashing. "I did. Once or twice when they started... but there was nobody on the other end." I can just see her picking up the call and shrugging it off when no one answered. Didn't I do the same thing the first time?

"There was," I say. My jaw clenching in anger. "Your phone was going off in the middle of the night last night. I answered it." Rage seeps through my body at the memory of the breathing and the grunt I heard. "I heard a man breathing and when I said 'hello' it startled him like he wasn't expecting me."

Lilah squints at me, confusion, disbelief and anger competing for control of her delicate features.

"Lilah, someone is stalking you. The calls and my car, that's not a coincidence."

Tears fill her eyes. "Oh shit," she whispers. "This is my fault." All the emotions I've been watching her battle disappear.

"No, Princess. It's not your fault. You didn't know."

Her face crumples. "No, but my brothers said they thought someone tampered with my Jeep battery. I didn't take it seriously. I thought they were just being paranoid. If I had listened..."

"Stop," I tell her firmly. I pull her into my arms. "There's nothing you could have done."

That's not entirely true. Had I known about the Jeep I would have gotten to the bottom of the phone calls right away but telling her that won't change our situation.

"Look, I need to check some things in my office..." I pause because there's no way around telling her the truth, even if this isn't how I wanted to do it. "Can you please come sit with me?"

I bring one of my kitchen chairs to the office and set it in front of my computer, pushing my comfy leather chair to the side for Lilah to sit in. She eyes me warily, and the sight of her distrust hits me right in the gut.

I sign in and pull up my security camera. The current feed shows a grainy image of Lilah's front yard, driveway, and front stoop. It only takes a second before it clicks and she opens her mouth, no doubt ready to unleash hell on me.

"Before you get mad," I say holding up a hand, begging for a little patience. "I had these before you moved in. I only use them to keep an eye on my own property, but after we found your door open, I moved them to watch your house. Just in case."

Lilah's looks at the screen through narrowed eyes, lips parted. Her cheeks are flushed and blotchy, anger practically seeping out of her. She takes a deep breath and says, "You've been watching me. For weeks." Her voice is *almost* calm, but I can hear the anger bubbling just beneath the surface.

"No, I had the cameras on your house in case something happened. I've been with you every night, here and over there. Since nothing else unusual happened, I never looked at the footage, I swear. I just didn't want someone hurting you."

Lilah looks placated but not happy, and she speaks through gritted teeth when she says, "You should have told me. If you'd been honest about it, I

128

wouldn't have minded so much. Besides, if you'd kept them facing your own property, *like you should have*, we'd be able to see who vandalized your car."

She still won't look at me as I try to apologize. "I know. And I'm sorry." I really am. I know I should have told her before now but trying to explain the cameras was going to bring up more questions. I click through the timeline as she sits next to me in silence.

"Stop!" she yells, smacking me on the arm. I stop the footage and back up slowly. A shadow crosses the bottom of the frame at 3:18am. The shadow moves on and off frame for several minutes. I think we can be reasonably certain that's the jackass who destroyed my car. We watch as the shadow moves until suddenly a figure dressed in black steps into the frame. The only thing that's clear is they have a black hoodie pulled up over their head. It looks like they have a slim build, but it's hard to judge height or anything else.

I'm livid. The thought of this piece of shit walking around my property, close enough to hurt Lilah, has me shaking with rage. Lilah places a hand on my arm, and her gentle touch is enough to calm my thunderous thoughts.

That is, until the figure crosses the yard and peeks in Lilah's front kitchen window before skulking around to the back.

Leave, I pray silently. *Please, just leave.*

But he doesn't leave. A minute later, a flashlight beam flashes from behind the blinds inside her bedroom window. Lilah gasps and grips my forearm, her fingernails digging into my skin as she covers her mouth with her other hand.

"Oh my god," she whispers.

Despite her frustration and anger with me, she lets me pull her into my lap. I wrap my arms around her as we silently watch the little light dim and move to another room.

After a couple minutes, the figure reappears outside, slinking back around the side of the house, disappearing towards the street. I fast forward a couple seconds at a time, but there's nothing else. I turn off the video, saving the clip to my hard drive and cloud storage. I don't know how much it will

129

help, but I'll look through it again later.

Lilah sits in my lap, her shoulders hunched miserably. I put a hand on her cheek, looking at her. She's pale, and I'm a little worried she might vomit. Her green eyes look glassy and she's staring vacantly at the screen. I wish I could absorb her pain, siphon it all away.

"Wait," she says, finally turning to look at me. "Why do you even have these cameras in the first place?"

There it is. My girl isn't stupid.

"That's... the other thing I need to tell you," I say as I look down at my hands. I hate myself right now. I've kept this from her so long and now I have no choice but to break it to her when she's already hurting. If I had just been a goddamn man about it and told her weeks ago, we might have prevented all of this from happening.

"My sister Ella..." I start. Fuck, this is hard. Lilah listens, still perched on my thigh, her back stiff and straight as a board.

"When I was 21, Ella married this prick she met in college. My dad didn't like the guy much, but he couldn't stop her. They moved to El Paso just after the wedding. I was still doing my time working for the FBI. I was so self-absorbed that I didn't realize how hard it was to get ahold of her until the next Christmas when she didn't come home to see us. She told us she couldn't make it, but she wouldn't say why or even answer her phone when we tried to call her."

Lilah's eyebrows draw together. As close as she is with her siblings, I'm sure she's imagining the worry that would cause.

"We didn't hear from her for days and then I got a call from her. She called me on a borrowed phone. All she said was she needed me to pick her up at a bus stop in North Austin before she hung up. My dad and I raced out to pick her up. When we found her--"

My voice breaks, my chest ripping apart all over again at the memory of my big sister, slumped in a bus stop waiting area. She had the hood of her coat pulled up and she was hugging herself. Even from across the room I could see the bruises, the dried blood on her forehead.

130

"She was in bad shape. We took her to the hospital, and they said she had three cracked ribs, a concussion, minor facial fractures. The hospital called the police and Ella told them everything while we watched. She couldn't make eye contact with anyone. She told me later how humiliating it all was. She's smart. She came from a good home. She had an education. She felt like she should have known better."

Lilah smooths her hands over my arm and over the muscles of my clenched fists. I watch the way her delicate fingers stroke my skin, focusing on that little motion to calm myself. It's been ten years, but I think a hundred could go by and I would still be filled with rage about what my sister went through.

"We *all* should have known better, but not one of us caught the warning signs. Ella's husband isolated her once they moved to El Paso. He emotionally abused her, she said. Little things at first but escalating until Ella demanded they spend Christmas at home in Austin. She was planning to use the trip to get help, but he refused and when she pushed back, he snapped. He beat her half to death."

Tears are streaming down Lilah's face when I look back up at her.

"I'm so sorry," she whispers. Her green eyes search mine like she's trying to assess the cracks in my soul so she can patch me back up.

"The police took a report. They kept calling it a domestic dispute. Can you believe that? They were useless. Worse than useless. Her husband had family ties in El Paso. They pulled a bunch of strings and, in the end, he was only charged with "Simple Assault." A class B misdemeanor. He did 60 days in jail and paid a $2,000 fine. That's it."

Lilah curses softly under her breath.

"He called her daily while he was in prison, not that she answered, but he wouldn't stop. His release date got closer and closer, and Ella started panicking. She knew he wouldn't leave her alone. She wanted to leave town, start over somewhere, but we didn't want her out there on her own."

"Part of my plea agreement with the FBI was that I agreed not to hack anything that wasn't assigned to me by my superiors. I'd followed the rules for years, but I wasn't about to let Ella's tormenter walk free after what he'd done..."

Lilah's eyes grow larger in her face.

"Oh god, Ben. What did you do?"

I laugh, but it comes out cold and humorless.

"Honestly? A lot less than I thought I'd have to."

Chapter 30: Lilah

I feel numb. Or at least my body does. My head is a swirling mess of emotions, disconnected from a body that can't keep up.

Ben laughs low and mirthless, as his eyes shift sideways, and he scrubs a hand down his face for about the tenth time this morning.

"I wanted him to go away, but that wasn't happening as long as his crimes were local and his family had the influence to talk things down. When I hacked him, I really thought I'd have to plant something." Ben shrugs, his arm still around me. "I was prepared to manufacture enough evidence to get the bastard put away for life, but it was all right there. He didn't even try very hard to hide it. The smug shit."

Ben shudders, and I'm suddenly very sure I don't want to know what he saw. "You can skip the details," I say.

Ben rubs a hand up my back. "There was plenty for the Justice Department to get involved, but what really sealed the deal were his financials. In the end, most of his jail time is from bank fraud, tax evasion and money laundering."

"How long did he get?" I ask.

"Sixty-five years."

"Good. What a rat bastard," I say. I don't know Ella well. I've only spoken to her a couple of times when she called Ben and I was in the room, but I already adore her.

Ben chuckles, sounding a little more like himself, but he stops when I ask, "Why are you telling me this now?"

"Because I didn't do it just the once," he whispers as he runs his fingers over the back of my hand. "I've helped-- I've been helping women in bad situations, people like my sister, disappear for years. Some of them had to start whole new lives. I've probably hacked into every government system in the country ten times over to help them do it."

I think about it for a second and honestly, the idea of Ben hacking a DMV or whatever to help someone live a safe life doesn't really bother me that much. I shrug as I search his eyes.

"Ok. I mean yeah, you're breaking the rules but it's for the right reasons, right?"

Ben swallows audibly.

"That's... still not all. I outed a senator last month for sexually harassing his subordinates and taking bribes."

I backhand his chest, not hard, but fast enough to catch him off guard. He makes an "oof" sound as I half yell, "That was you?! I read about that! The bastard got what he deserved if you ask me."

Ben grins. "He probably deserved worse. But Lilah, I do that kind of stuff all the time."

"Aren't you worried you'll get caught?" I ask. The thought of him being arrested and taken away from me is terrifying.

"Honestly, not really. In my experience, nobody complains when you take down a terrible person. The authorities concerned don't look too hard when someone anonymously sends them all the evidence they need to do their job. Plus, I'm really good at covering my tracks. If worse came to worst, I still have contacts in the FBI that owe me huge favors."

Something about all of this is still making my stomach churn. I've got a headache and my chest is squeezing uncomfortably. There's something icky about charging desperate women money to help them.

"Is this how you make money?" I ask. "Were you lying about the corporate jobs you were doing?"

"God no," he replies vehemently. "I really make my money off the corporate stuff. I don't charge for the... the gray area stuff."

The tension in my chest eases a bit. "I'd ask you why you do it, but I think I get it. No one should have to go through what your sister went through." His fingertips flex against the small of my back and a small, hopeful smile turns the corners of his mouth up.

134

I try to figure out what's eating at me, talking my way through it. "I don't care about the legality. I really don't. People like that deserve to be punished, but... I wish you would have trusted me with this."

Ben meets my eyes, and he looks tortured. He opens his mouth to say something, but I hold up my finger.

"I'm not finished," I say, pushing away from his chest and standing. I already feel the loss of his strong arms around me, but the distance between us is much colder than just the loss of body heat. He stays sitting, letting me have the upper hand, at least for now.

"You got your turn to talk and now it's mine. I *told* you how hard it is for me to let people in. I flat out told you. And you still pushed your way in, feeding me half-truths and lying through omission the whole time."

I've found the thread of hurt that's needling me and when I pull it, a hole rips through my chest, spilling out all the things I need to say.

"You pushed me to trust you, but you were never honest with me. You didn't even give me a chance. And why?! Did you think I couldn't handle it? That I'd shake my finger at you or turn you in for helping people that couldn't do it for themselves?! Did you think so little of me?"

To be fair, Ben never tries to backpedal. Never interrupts or argues. He just sits there, watching me, listening to me rail against him, his face miserable. I should feel sorry for him, but the anger is climbing in me.

The unfairness. The hypocrisy of making me trust him when he didn't have the decency to return the favor. How many times did I come home and ask him what he did that day, only for him to lie to my face? *Omit*, I remind myself. It wasn't all lies. He just hid an immense piece of himself while carving me open and claiming my heart.

A couple nights ago we laid in bed, half asleep. He stroked my hair, listening to me as I recalled the little pieces of my mom and dad that I remembered from my childhood. "I've never told anyone that," I'd said. I felt so close to him. So vulnerable. And now? Now I feel like such a fool because he could have told me then, but he didn't. I sort through a hundred other moments that he could have told me, and he didn't say a damn word. Not until he absolutely had to.

I shiver, my jaw clenched, as I roll my shoulders. I'd hulk out and flip his desk if I wasn't 5'2" with all the raw, threatening power of a Carebear. I wish I had an expensive glass of wine to throw at the wall. I bet the shattering glass and wine dripping down the paint would be satisfying as hell right now.

How did this morning go so far off the rails? An hour ago, I was planning breakfast and a lazy day with Ben. Now I'm imagining destroying his office just to soothe my anger. I need to get out of here. But I can't go back to my fucking house, now can I? Not when someone has been in there, touching my things and doing god knows what. Bile rises in my throat as I fight back that train of thought. I literally can't go there yet. I want to go home, but Ben is the only place that feels like home.

Felt like home. Tears are sliding down my face, landing hot and wet on the front of my shirt. I'm not even sure when they started, but Ben stands, cupping my face in his hands, brushing my tears off my cheeks with his thumbs.

"I'm so sorry, Lilah. Truly, I--" His voice is wracked with emotion, but I push his hands away. He feels so good, but I know that if I let him touch me now, he'll make my anger melt away and I am not ready to let go of this.

"I need to go," I say as I turn and leave the room. I beat him to the kitchen, sweeping my belongings back into my purse and heading for the front door. He follows me silently.

"Lilah. No. Stay here." It's not a request. His voice is commanding and if I wasn't so pissed off, I'd probably be turned on as hell right now. Too bad for Ben I'm ready to spit nails.

"How dare you?!" I yell, whipping around to face him. "How dare you make demands right now?! This," I say, gesturing back and forth between him, "was just sex. And now it's over." I regret the words as soon as they fly out of my mouth but turn away and open the door without apologizing.

Ben's enormous hand hits the door before I can open it more than a few inches and he leans on it with all of his body weight, slamming it shut again. He doesn't touch me, but he uses his massive frame to cage me in as I turn to

136

face him. I'm afraid I'll see rage burning in his eyes.

But when my eyes meet his, there's no anger or violence. All I see is desperate tenderness. And hurt. I may have gone too far with that parting shot.

"I'll let you go in a minute, I promise," he says softly. "But you're not leaving like that. This isn't just sex. You and I both know this is more than that. I made a mistake and I'm sorry. If you need some space, that's ok. But I love you and I'm not letting you leave thinking I did this to hurt you."

I search his face as the blood pumps through my brain, thundering and blocking out rational thought. I give him a hard look, at war with myself on how to respond, but Ben opens the door for me, and I storm out.

He loves me? And this is how he tells me? The shitty cynical side of my brain is accusing him of saying it to manipulate me, but the rational side is fighting for control. Its squeaky little voice is all too happy to remind me that the look on his face was sincere. That voice gets louder and louder as I stomp across our respective front yards and get into my Jeep.

Ben is still watching me from his front door, leaning one hand on the door frame. The other is running its way through his curls. I eye him and debate going back and letting him wrap me up in his big muscular arms. I just need a minute to breathe and some room to think.

Chapter 31: Ben

Watching Lilah drive away while doing nothing to stop her is one of the most gut-wrenching things I've ever experienced. I told her I love her, and she walked away. Well, huffed away. Fuck me and my big mouth. That wasn't the time or place to blurt that out. God knows if I'll ever be able to fix the damage I just did. I resist the urge to slam the door. I resist a lot of urges, like smashing everything in my house and calling her frantic, begging her to come back.

I know she needs time to cool off and process but I hate this. I hate letting her leave, but I have to give Lilah some credit. She's strong, and she's forgiving. She's kind and intelligent. She'll come around if I give her some time to work through her anger. In the meantime, I can be productive.

Hacking phone companies is unbelievably easy. Within minutes of sitting down at my computer, I'm in the system and looking through Lilah's phone records. It's one more breach of trust I'll have to apologize for, but this is necessary. I am going to track down that stalking bastard and ruin his life so thoroughly he'll be lucky to have a gutter to sleep in when I'm done.

There's a number hidden behind the blocked caller ID that traces to a prepaid phone. I swear to god, the number of people who think a prepaid phone can't be traced is staggering. The SIM card identification tracks to a purchase at a local electronics store. I shake my head as I pull up the credit card information and check the clock. Thirty-seven minutes. That's all the time it takes to track down the identity of Lilah's dumb ass stalker. The purchase records show a credit card purchase dated almost three months ago and the name Nelson, T.

Hacking a major credit card website is marginally more difficult than a big box retailer and it takes me a couple minutes to access the account of one Terrance Nelson of Guerneville, California. The name rattles around in my head. I can't place it, but I know I've heard it before. I scroll through the purchase records. Most of it is benign shit. Drive through tacos, drugstore and grocery charges, a little online shopping... but one purchase stands out:

$178 to ISpySupplyLLC a little over two months ago.

A quick search for the company pulls up one of the slimiest websites I've ever had the displeasure of viewing. Trackers, mini listening bugs, nanny cams and other devices specifically marketed for sleaze-balls to spy on and record women without their knowledge. They don't even have the decency to advertise it for catching a cheating spouse. No. They're using phrases like "She'll never know!" "See what she *REALLY* does in private!" and "What she doesn't know won't hurt her!"

I'm in a hurry to figure out what this douchebag ordered, otherwise I would out every single one of this website's clients to their mothers and bosses before burning this shit to the ground. As it stands, I'll have to come back to it later.

The invoice for T. Nelson only has one item, but as I read it my lip pulls back in a twitching snarl. A magnetic GPS tracker for a car. I feel like hot tar is pumping through my veins. I hope the police get to this packet of dick sauce before I do, otherwise I might just kill him.

I run a quick search for him on social media and pull up a page for Terrance Nelson in Sonoma County. A greasy weasel of a man looks back at me from the cover photo. Something fires up in my memories. I know I've seen him before but can't quite place it. Scrolling through the "About" section, it finally clicks.

"Works at: Manager at Blue Ruin Speakeasy."

"Son of a bitch," I mutter as it falls into place. Weasel Face is the manager that was giving Lilah a hard time the first night we met. She's told me a little about him. He was the reason she left the bar. He kept pursuing her after she told him no. Over and over.

Piece of shit.

I need to get into his computer, but it's going to have to wait. I need to find Lilah and make sure she's safe first. And I need to warn her.

I screen shot everything I found as I tap my phone screen to call Lilah. My breath sticks in my chest as I wait to hear her voice on the other end. "This is Lilah! Leave a message."

"Fuck!" I yell as I remember her phone, power off, sitting in my fridge.

If Terry is tracking her car, he knows exactly where she is and I'm sitting here like a fucking idiot with no way to reach her. I rub my temples and stare at the wall. Where would she go? Her Gran's house is an obvious choice, but I think of her sister's bakery. As close as she is with Olive, I'd put my money on the bakery.

I run for the front door as I search for the bakery phone number, grabbing my keys and dashing out the front door. I'm in the driveway when I remember the slashed tires on my car. It's sitting like a pathetic heap on the pavement.

"Double-fucking-fuckity-fuck-fuck!"

Chapter 32: Lilah

As I drive, I try to wrap my head around this whole morning. My mind keeps repeating things over and over and over. From the footage of the man entering my house, to Ben's vandalized car, to his confessions...

My heart hurts.

I'm angry.

I feel dirty and violated at the thought of someone skulking through my house, touching god knows what. I'm going to have to burn everything I own and start over somewhere fresh.

As I mull things over, I wonder if I might have been a little unfair to Ben. His confession was a lot to take in, but would I have flown off the handle like that if I wasn't already upset about the video of the stalker? Probably not.

I still would have been hurt, though.

This was a huge secret to keep from me. Sure, we've only been seeing each other for a few weeks and it's not like he knows every single thing about me. And I suppose he can't just go blabbing that hacking stuff around to every person he meets. I'm not a lawyer, but I'm fairly certain he'd go to prison for a long ass time if he got caught.

I shudder at the thought of Ben in a prison jumpsuit. No matter what happens between us, I'll protect his secret.

I wonder how many women he's helped. How many predators and abusers has he stopped? If he was telling the truth, he's making the world a better, safer place. Maybe his methods are a little… morally ambiguous. But I bet the people he's helped and protected along the way don't care.

I've been driving aimlessly but end up outside Olive Branch Bakery. I pull in and park in the back next to the dumpsters. Olive isn't expecting me, but I could use a coffee and a hug from my sister. I'll make it quick; I decide. And then I'll go back and talk to Ben.

I unbuckle my seatbelt and grab my purse. As I pick it up, I see the little black box I found under my Jeep yesterday. Jesus, was that really just yesterday? I set my purse back down, picking up the box and rolling it around in my hands as I take another look at it. A cold weight sinks in my stomach for like the tenth time today.

How stupid can I be? Yesterday, I wondered why a car part would be magnetic instead of wired in. The short answer is, it wouldn't be. I am a fucking idiot. A naïve, trusting idiot. If someone is bold enough to break into my house, they're sure as shit bold enough to stick a tracker on my car.

I should call the police, but I can't tell them about the video without talking to Ben. I need to make sure I don't say the wrong thing and land him in trouble.

Ben.

I should call Ben. I bet dollars to donuts he could figure out who bought it and stuck it on my car before the police even finished filing a report. After what he said, and the way I left, I feel sick to my stomach. Just thinking about the look on his face when I drove away is enough to break my heart. I can't believe I said that it was just sex. Way over the line.

I need to call him, like, right now. I need to tell him what a dummy I was, and I need to apologize my face off. I dig around in my purse looking for my phone only to realize that I left it in Ben's fridge. A little growl escapes my throat as I remember the way I stormed out while my phone languished next to Ben's bacon.

I need to go inside and use the phone, but I don't know what to do with the box. If it really is a tracker, and I'm pretty sure it is, I really want to huck it into the nearest body of water. But then Ben couldn't use it to figure out who put it on my car, and I wouldn't be able to hand it over to the police or file a report. I can't throw it away, but I also *really* don't want to carry it inside. It feels tainted.

I could hide it behind the dumpsters, I reason. No one will mess with it there, and if anyone is paying attention to its location, it would look like it's still in the parking lot. It's marginally better than keeping it in my possession or leaving it in my Jeep. The whole situation sucks so hard. Tears are welling in my eyes again, borne of the helplessness of the situation. I'm overwhelmed

142

and frustrated, and I feel like a dick for the way I treated Ben.

This is all so stupid. I was stupid. I want Ben. Just Ben and nobody else. And I really want to apologize for storming off after he told me he loves me. That was so shitty of me.

I let my frustration and anger takeover, and sob into my hands for a minute before pulling myself together. I need to deal with everything that has gone wrong this morning, starting with the stupid fucking tracker.

"Suck it up, Lilah." I mutter to myself as I brush the tears from my face. Taking the black box, I hop out of the car and scoot around the narrow space between the dumpster and privacy fence. I tuck the box on a little rail that sticks out behind the dumpster. The magnet thunks into the metal, keeping it secure. There. I'll come back for it once Ben gets here.

I've got this, I think as I turn and brush my hands down my hips. *This is fine*.

At least it would be, if there wasn't a man standing at the end of the dumpster, blocking my way. Startled and already on edge, I let out a scream before I can stop myself. My fear turns to anger when I realize I recognize the man.

"Terry?" I ask. "What are you doing here?" He might be the absolute last person I want to see right now.

"I've been worried about you," he says in a calm voice, as if it's perfectly reasonable for someone to sneak up on a former employee behind a bunch of trash.

"Right... well, I'm fine," I say as I gesture for him to let me by. He pretends like he didn't see it and holds his position. A heavy dread spreads through my limbs and I feel like I'm going to be sick.

"Why did you quit the bar? We never see each other anymore." He smiles, but it doesn't reach his eyes. The dead-eyed way he watches me coupled with his flat tone gives me the willies. I don't think I ever realized how empty his eyes look until this moment.

"My sister needed more help here at the bakery. It sucks, but family first.

You know how it is. She's probably looking for me. I should head inside, but it was great seeing you." I play dumb and force out a cheerful smile, even though I already know the truth. It was Terry. The calls, my battery, Ben's car, and the goddamn tracker. It was all Terry and I'm about five seconds from throwing up on his stupid wingtip shoes.

Unfortunately, I'm not much of an actress and he isn't buying the innocent act. His lips pull up to the side in a sneer.

"Don't be cute. I know it was your boyfriend who threatened me last night. I just wanted to talk to you, but he flew off the handle. He's dangerous. You shouldn't trust him. I tried to warn him. You deserve better." I catch a whiff of Terry's bargain basement cologne mixed with the dumpster smell while he's talking, and it's all I can do to keep the bile down. He should get an award for the sleaziest stalker.

"Slashing tires isn't a warning, it's a threat," I retort. I should keep my mouth shut. I really should. The last thing I need is for him to go crazy. Crazier, I mentally amend.

Terry takes a step towards me, a flash of anger in his cold eyes. I could just fucking kick myself. I'm not going to get out of this by mouthing off. I can't push past him, and I'm probably not going to win any physical encounters. He may be slim, but he still has a good eight inches on me. I might be scrappy, but we're tied at best.

Scenarios frantically flash through my head and I am kicking myself for leaving my purse in my Jeep. My pepper spray is like six feet away and completely useless. Julia is going to be so salty with me about that.

The only chance I have is to sweet talk him. Lure him in and sneak attack. As I hold out a hand, trying to keep him at arm's length while giving him the softest look I can muster.

"I'm sorry, I shouldn't have said that. It was just surprising, you know. Just talk to me. It's just the two of us here." Boy, am I painfully aware that it's just the two of us. Unless someone decides to take out the trash, which is doubtful at this time of day, no one is coming to rescue me.

Terry looks placated but holds his ground. "You were supposed to be mine. I can't let him steal you. It's not fair!" His voice cracks, rising in volume. "I'm a nice guy and I *deserve* you. He's just a big meathead but you couldn't see past his stupid square jaw!"

My hands are shaking, but I do my best to hide the terror he's causing. I have to keep him calm and I get the distinct impression he won't like it if I act scared right now.

"You're right, Terry, but he and I are through. I broke up with him this morning."

This better be convincing as fuck.

"Do you really care about me that much?" I ask him, forcing a small smile. "I've never had someone stand up for me like that."

"Yeah?" he asks, surprise and hope lifting his face a little. I'm not sure what part he's replying to, but I really don't give a flying fart. He's calmer, and he's smiling back at me.

"Yeah," I tell him. "Maybe we could try this," I say. "I could make you dinner at my house. Wouldn't that be nice?"

"Really?" A maniacal grin is crawling up his face.

This has to work.

I have to get away.

"Yeah..." I say. I step closer to him and reach a hand out. The smell of his greasy hair is making me nauseous. *Soft look,* I tell myself. *Adoring eyes. Don't gag.*

Terry is frozen. I don't think he accounted for me initiating contact. *Keep it together. Keep it together. Keep it together.* The phrase is my lifeline and I chant it in my head over and over as I put my arms around his neck. I'm so close I can feel his breath on my face. Just when I thought he couldn't get any more repulsive, I realize that he smells like fish sticks.

"L-Lilah," he stammers.

I don't hear the rest of what he would have said because I pull my leg back and slam it up into his balls, channeling that one free trial kickboxing class I took.

Terry falls to the ground, cupping his junk with both hands. I don't stay to watch my handiwork. Kneework? Whatever. I jump around him and sprint for the side door of the bakery.

"You fucking bitch!" I hear him scream behind me. My heart is pumping so hard I feel like it might explode. I chance a look back, but he's still on the ground, curled in the fetal position like the pathetic man-child he is. Good. I hope I did permanent damage. Just as I turn back towards the bakery, the side door opens and Luis steps out looking panicked. He sees me and his eyes grow wide.

"Lilah, what is going on out here? Are you ok?" He catches me as I run into him, flour puffs off his apron into the surrounding air. My body is trembling with adrenaline and fear, but I've never been more grateful to see him in my life. Luis holds my upper arms, supporting me and holding me in place.

"He cornered me," I gulp a breath as I point back to the dumpsters. "He's crazy... been stalking me."

Luis' jaw sets in a hard line. "Go inside, Lilah. Lock the door, call the police."

I try to pull him in with me, but he gently pushes me towards the door. "Call the police. I'm just going to make sure he stays put."

146

Chapter 33: Ben

I *might* have demanded Mr. Miller give me his car keys. It's not so much a carjacking as it is a... less-than-willing auto lending. I call the bakery as I drive. It rings twice before a chipper voice answers. "Olive Branch Bakery, can you hold please?"

"No!" I yell into the phone, but they've already switched lines and I'm left swearing into the void. "Come on," I chant. I'm only a few minutes from the bakery but I wait on hold just in case they pick up again before I get there. Soft music is still playing when I pull into the front of the bakery, wincing as the car bottoms out on the parking lot entrance. I might need to apologize to Mr. Miller. I end the call as I run up the front steps.

Searching the dining room, I think I see Lilah at a table in the corner. A glance up in my direction sends my heart plummeting. It's not Lilah. It's her sister, Olive. The look on my face must be enough to alarm her because her eyebrows scrunch up and she tilts her head. She looks so much like Lilah. The panic is rising up in me and I hate that I don't know where Lilah is.

Olive excuses herself, leaving a couple at the table to go through a notebook.

"Have you seen Lilah?" I ask.

Her confused look turns darker. "Not today, why?"

"Have you seen Terry, Lilah's boss from the bar hanging around?"

"Ew, no. Why?"

Ignoring her question, I head back towards the kitchen. Maybe she's back there? I'm grasping at straws, but I don't care. Olive follows me and smacks me on the arm hard enough to hurt but not derail me.

"Excuse you! I asked you a question. What is going on?"

It's not exactly my story to tell, but fuck it, it's not like Lilah would keep it a secret from her sister, anyway. "He's been stalking her," I say as I walk into the kitchen, checking the supply closet on the way.

"What are you talking about?!" Olive's voice sounds panicked, but I don't have time to explain it because Lilah comes flying in the side door. Relief washes over me, but it's short lived when I take in the tear tracks on her cheeks, the pallor of her skin, and the fear in her eyes.

"Ben!" Lilah shrieks as she runs and jumps into my arms. I catch her, sweeping her up in my arms. Nothing in this world can compare to the feeling of holding her. I bury my hand in her hair, cupping the back of her head and hold her against my chest.

"Ben, it's Terry. It was all him," she tells me.

"I know, Princess. I figured it out after--"

"No, you don't understand. He's here. He's outside. He cornered me behind the dumpsters- tried to - I kicked him..." She's shaking like a leaf. "I need to call the police."

Olive acts before the rest of us, snatching a phone off the wall and dialing 9-1-1. Her eye is twitching as she looks at me over Lilah's head, murder in her eyes. I suspect she'd be game to help me bury a body if it meant protecting her sister.

Lilah looks up at me. "Can you check on Luis? He's outside. He wanted to make sure Terry didn't get away."

The last thing in the world I want to do right now is leave her side, but the expression on her face is heart wrenching. I hold her face in my hands and bend down to kiss her. Our lips brush and I feel her sigh, relaxing into me. It's over in a second. I let her go with a painful twist in my chest. It feels wrong to leave her, but she needs to know Luis is safe and I'll do anything to make her feel better. Olive reaches out and pulls Lilah to her, shooing me out the door as she answers questions for the dispatcher.

I jog out the door to the parking lot, where I find Luis leaning casually against a dumpster. A familiar, ferrety looking man is weeping openly at his feet. He's holding his balls, a nasty black eye blossoming under a split eyebrow. Lilah said she kicked the guy, but a quick glance at Luis' right hand, the knuckles bloodied, explains the black eye.

"Can you believe this chuckle fuck attacked me?" Luis says in an

148

outraged voice.

"He really should have known better," I reply darkly, shaking my head. Terrance sneers at me as I approach the two of them. I squat next to him, my body shaking with rage. I can hear sirens getting closer, but I want to make sure he hears this before they take him away. He threatened my Lilah, the first and only woman I'll fall in love with. He terrified the woman I'm going to spend the rest of my life with.

I grab his hair and yank his head back. "You are so fucking lucky the police are coming, you pathetic little snake. If I had my way, they'd never find your body. You are going to confess to all of it. You will plead guilty, without dragging this through a trial. If you don't, know that I can make your life a living hell no matter where they put you. I can ruin you and your entire family without blinking an eye. You damn well better remember that. If I hear even a whisper of your bullshit, I'll make good on my threat to rip your balls off and feed them to you. Cool?" I say, clapping a hand on his shoulder. He flinches and cries harder, but nods.

I stand as the first police car pulls into the lot. Luis and I stand aside as an officer cuffs Terrance, reading him his rights as he pats him down. Lilah and Olive step outside as Terrance is dragged to his feet and frogmarched to a cruiser.

It takes forever to file the police report, but Lilah leans against my side, letting me hold her close as we tell them the (slightly abridged) version of the phone calls and discovering the vandalism to my car. Lilah points the officers to the tracker that she left behind the dumpsters. She carefully leaves out my less-than-legal work, but I offer up the footage of Terrance entering her house. Anything to extend his prison sentence.

Lilah is incredible. She keeps her shit together, making sure she gives them every detail she can remember. She tells them how he cornered her and how she sweet-talked him to get close enough to knee him in the cajones. Just listening to her retell it makes my blood boil, but the female officer cracks a tiny grin and winces as she whispers, "Nice."

Lilah refuses medical attention every time I bring it up. After the tenth time, she smacks me on the chest. "It's not like his squishy little balls hurt my knee," she says. "Really, I'm fine. I just want to go lie down and take a nap. I'll be good as new, I promise."

"Not in your house," I say, disgustedly thinking of the video footage from last night.

"Ew," she says with a shudder. "I never want to set foot in that house again. Except... I need to get Frankie."

"Stay with me," I tell her quietly. I'm all too aware that we didn't leave things in a great place this morning. I also don't want to pressure her after everything she's been through today, but the thought of letting her go anywhere without me is unbearable.

Lilah's eyes are large in her face as she searches mine and then nods. I feel a little swell of hope, and for the first time since she left this morning, I take a real breath.

The officer gives us a sympathetic smile, "We'll need to investigate the break-in at your house, but an officer can go with you if you need to collect a pet and some clothes." Lilah nods and the officer talks into her radio asking someone to escort us. I give Olive and Luis my phone number before we leave. Lilah's phone is still in my fridge and even if the police don't want it, I don't want Lilah to carry it until I know for a fact there isn't any spyware on it.

Lilah leaves her Jeep with the police and rides with me. We drive most of the way in silence. I lace my fingers through hers and rest our hands on her thigh while she leans her head back, staring at the ceiling of the car. There's so much to say, but it's a quick trip. I don't think either of us wants to get into it until we're really alone.

It's only when we turn into our neighborhood that she straightens up and looks around. "Wait, whose car is this?" she asks with a laugh.

"Fred Miller's," I tell her with a grin.

"He let you drive it?" she asks me skeptically.

"I'm not sure I'd describe it that way. I asked nicely, but he wasn't big on the idea until I threatened to send pictures of his dog crapping on everyone's lawns around to the neighborhood group."

Lilah laughs softly. "I love that you'd threaten a salty geriatric for me."

"There is *nothing* I wouldn't do for you, Princess." My voice cracks a little as I speak, and I have to clear my throat to hold back a wave of emotion.

She gives my hand a gentle squeeze in response, and it's all I can do not to pull over and pull her into my lap. I'm afraid that if I give into my need to hold her, I won't be able to let go and we'll be sleeping in this ancient Buick for days.

When I turn onto our street, we're greeted by half a dozen squad cars, all parked in front of our houses. Police tape stretches around the perimeter of Lilah's house and my car. Photographs are being taken, notebooks jotted in, and it seems the neighbors couldn't pass up the entertainment. There's a buzz of activity on the outside of the tape, Mr. Miller in the center of it all. He stands on the sidewalk, craning his neck to see what's going on while gossiping with some other neighbors.

He sees me coming and marches over with his hand out for his keys. He snatches them out of my hand, clearly torn between telling me off and nosing for details. I thank him, pushing down the impulse to hug him because I know he'd hate it. Coerced or not, if it wasn't for his help, I wouldn't have been there when Lilah needed me. His dog can shit in my yard anytime it wants. I'll never hold a grudge about it again.

Chapter 34: Lilah

The whole scene should make me upset. People traipsing in and out of my house, going through my things, the fact that my house is an active crime scene... and yet I really don't care. Terry is going to prison and I know my Ben will do whatever it takes to keep him away from me for the rest of my life.

A young officer shakes my hand and lifts the crime scene tape for Ben and me to duck under. Admittedly, it was much easier for me to sneak under the yellow tape. Ben's shoulder snags it and rips it, making me laugh. He ties it back together with the officer's help and gives me an apologetic smile.

He puts a possessive hand on my lower back as we walk inside. The weight of it is warm and protective, and despite everything else we've been through in the last few hours, I feel safe.

"Are you ok?" Ben asks, looking around my entry way at the commotion inside.

"Yeah," I tell him honestly. "But I'd like to hurry up and get out of here." Ben nods and we work together quietly to pack up Frankie in her travel cage. Ben grabs the veggies out of my fridge for her while I get the water bowl. I'd be lying if I said I didn't scope a peek at his butt when he bent over to put the lettuce in a bag. He catches me and tosses me a wink. His winks usually send my panties into spontaneous melt down, but this one is a sweeter, more affectionate look than I expected.

Ben sets the bag down next to Frankie and pulls me into his chest. He holds me tight, his cheek resting on top of my head. I don't know how long we stand like that, but an officer clears her throat, as she moves by us with an embarrassed, "Excuse me."

Yeah, I do not want to spend another minute in this house.

I go to grab some clothes out of the closet, but I run a finger over one of the shirts. I don't know what Terry touched. I can't stand the idea of wearing anything until it's been washed. And maybe boiled. In acid.

Ben catches my hesitation, his brows pulling together for a second before he gets it. I don't have to say a word. He takes my hand and pulls me back out of the closet and down the hall. He grabs Frankie's stuff under one arm, holding her cage in one hand and lacing the fingers of his free hand back through mine.

Ben ignores the neighbors and the police outside. He doesn't even look at his butchered car as we cross our front yards to his house. He just determinedly marches the three of us to his front door. He unlocks it, pressing his hand to my lower back in that proprietary way of his. God, I love it when he takes charge. He locks the door behind us before setting Frankie down and walking through the living areas, closing all the curtains.

I watch him, frozen in place. I feel disconnected from my body and I wonder if maybe I'm a little shell-shocked. The quiet of the house is oppressive after all the sirens and radios. Ben seems determined to charge ahead, setting Frankie up with some water and putting food in her cage.

"Ben," I say.

"Do you want something to eat?" he asks. I haven't eaten, but I'm not hungry.

"No, but Ben--"

"Do you want something to drink? You can take a shower if you want." Ben doesn't meet my eye, but he rambles as he pops another piece of lettuce into Frankie's cage. "Or I can fill up a bath for you. I don't have bubbles or anything." I place my hand on his and my heart aches when I realize he's shaking.

"Ben," I say firmly. "Ben, look at me." He glances up, his beautiful brown eyes haunted. I step into him, wrapping my arms around his middle. He cradles me against his chest.

"I'm so sorry." My voice is muffled against his chest and I breathe in the familiar, comforting scent of his shirt.

"Lilah..." His voice is gently chiding, and I know he's going to tell me I

153

didn't do anything wrong, but I need to say this.

"I'm so sorry for the way I left this morning," I plow ahead. "I never should have left like that." Ben runs his fingers through my hair, pressing his lips to the top of my head.

"I understand why you did," he whispers, holding me tighter. Of course, he understands. Ben gets me like nobody else, except maybe my sisters. Half the time I wonder if he's psychic with the way he can predict me.

"I--" his voice chokes and he clears his throat. "I was so scared I lost you. I can't imagine this world without you in it." His voice is ragged, his words vibrating through me. I can't imagine living without him either. I don't care that we've only been together a little while. I don't give a single fuck that he kept a secret from me. I need him like I need the air in my lungs. I love him and the rest is just details.

"Lilah, I swear I'll never keep--" I wiggle my way back in his arms, just enough so I can reach up to touch his face and put my fingers over his lips.

"You already apologized this morning and I forgive you." I run my fingers over his 24-hour shadow, loving the feel of the bristly hairs. He is devastatingly handsome, but underneath that, he's the most beautiful person I know. Giving him my heart is the easiest thing I've ever done because I know he'll protect it and treasure it over anything else.

"Here's what I should have said earlier. I don't know how you snuck into my heart, but I love you. I love you so much it hurts," I say through a hoarse throat.

Ben's eyes are intense, and full of adoration as he presses his forehead to mine. "I love you too," he says before pressing his lips to mine. After everything we've been through today, we pour the pent-up emotions into the kiss. All the frustration, anger, fear and heartbreak melts away as his lips move against mine, replaced by joy and relief.

My fingers wind under his shirt and the feel of his skin under my hands is almost more than I can bear. I can't keep my hands off him, kissing him harder. The soft rush of his breath against my mouth lights a fire in me. I could blame the adrenaline crash or the declarations of love, but Ben always

154

makes me crazy for him. A single look, a little touch, a kiss on the neck, and I am dying for him. Greedy for anything I can get.

He holds me close as we kiss and my nipples rub against his chest, tightening to aching points. His massive thigh presses between mine, and I'm helplessly lost as my hips roll against it. I moan into his kiss as I feel a rush of moisture between my thighs.

Ben's hand in my hair tightens, holding my head back to look at me. His eyes search mine, looking for something. "We can do this later," he says. "I'd understand if you need time after--"

"Fuck no," I say. "I need this. I need you and I do *not* want to wait." Ben grins at me, his grip on my hair firm. I blink up at him. "But I do feel kind of grimy. Maybe we can multitask in the shower?"

Ben growls and scoops me off my feet before I even finish the thought, carrying me to the bathroom. He reaches in to start the water before grabbing the back of his t-shirt and pulling it over his head. I watch him shamelessly as he unbuttons his jeans, the muscles in his stomach and arms flexing with every movement.

Mine. He's all mine, I think with a little shiver of joy.

"What are you grinning at, Princess?" he asks as he tosses his pants and boxers into the laundry hamper. His swollen cock bobs against his abdomen, demanding attention. He strokes it once, looking me up and down, blatant hunger in his eyes.

I shrug but smile harder. "I love you. It feels so good to say it out loud. I can't stop saying it now that we've broken the seal."

Ben stalks over to me, his hands landing on my hips as he kisses my neck. "I love you too," he says before biting my shoulder gently. His thumbs sneak under the hem of my shirt, his hands skating up my stomach and ribs as he lifts the shirt slowly. He pulls it over my head and throws it aside. His fingers stroke my collarbone and across the swell of my breasts as he steps behind me. His hard length presses into my backside as one hand slips under my bra, finding my nipple and rolling it with expert pressure. His other hand palms my stomach, slipping into the front of my jeans and teasing the edge of my panties.

I slip a hand up around the back of his neck and let my head rest on his chest as desire saps the tightness from my muscles. He unhooks my bra and flicks my jeans open as his breath whispers over my chest. I shimmy out of my jeans and Ben groans as I bend over in front of him to push them down, my ass pressing against his erection. As good as these skinny jeans look, they are a bitch to get out of.

It doesn't matter how silly I feel because the second I'm free of my clothes, Ben pulls me into the shower with him. His lips are on mine before I even feel the water. His tongue slides against mine, thick and hot. I moan into his mouth, the muffled sound vibrating through us. His possessive hands move over my body, caressing me like he's reassuring himself that I'm still all here.

Ben backs me into the tile wall, the cold surface pricks my skin. Goosebumps shiver their way up to my shoulder blades. He dips his head, drawing my nipple into his mouth, the graze of his teeth sending electricity sizzling through my body. My clit throbs, crying out for his attention. His large, rough hands grasp my hips, fingers pressing into my skin as his erection rocks against my belly.

"More," I gasp, my fingers laced in his hair.

Ben growls and straightens, hooking his forearms under my thighs and lifting me. I let out a squeak of surprise, wrapping my arms around his neck and clinging to him. I so rarely see him at eye level unless we're in bed, but it never gets old. He pins me to the wall with his body, holding me tight. His shaft presses against my entrance, the broad head stretching me as he slips inside.

Ben watches me through lust hooded eyes as he lowers me, slowly impaling me on his cock. I gasp as he fills me, sinking to the hilt. The muscle in his jaw ticks as he holds me in place, inching out before filling me again. Our bodies slick against each other, water sluicing between us as Ben thrusts in and out of me. I rock my hips against his hold, something lining up just right to make my eyes roll back in my head. He growls, chest heaving against my breasts as he keeps the pace achingly slow.

156

He presses his forehead to mine, his hair dripping water down his face that runs down his neck and chest in rivulets. "Whose girl are you?" he rumbles, his gaze burning into mine.

"Yours," I gasp. "I'm yours." His cock swells impossibly thicker inside me. He holds me firmly, possessing me with every stroke. My body is his and I fucking love it.

"That's right, Princess," he grunts, picking up speed. The wet slap of our bodies echoes off the tile as the steam swirls around us. His thumb finds my clit, rubbing it as he pounds into me. "You're my girl and I want to watch you fucking come. I want to feel your tight little pussy come all over my cock," he growls. "Give it to me, Princess. I need it." He ducks, his mouth clamping around my nipple. My vision blurs as the sensations assault me, rolling through me, fighting for attention. I can't hold back the small scream as my body explodes, pleasure gripping me roughly, wringing me out.

Ben comes, lips parted as every muscle in his body flexes. His throbbing cock pulses, twitching as he empties himself inside me. His head hits my shoulder as our bodies both go slack. He holds me a moment longer before letting my shaky feet find the floor.

Chapter 35: Ben

The water washes over us, starting to cool as the hot water runs out. I'm so grateful to have her soft curves pressed against me, I couldn't care less about the rest of the world. The smell of her skin, the feel of her fingertips on my biceps, her tiny frame trembling against me. I'd give anything for her.

Lilah laughs softly in my arms. "We forgot the condom."

My head snaps up. Fuck. I can't believe I did that. I was so lost in her; it didn't even cross my mind. I run my hand over my face.

"Jesus, I'm so sorry," I say to her, searching her face for anger, but for all my concern she's completely relaxed, smiling sweetly.

"It's fine. Birth control is a wonderful thing."

"Oh," I reply. That's a relief, right? I should be happy. I mean, I am, but I have the briefest flash of Lilah, carrying a smiling baby on her hip and maybe I'm a complete dick, but I like it. We towel off and for a moment, I try to push the thought out of my head. But then I remember everything that happened today, and I decide; I don't want to let that thought go. I want little babies with her green eyes. I want to put a ring on her finger. I want to spend every morning waking up with her in my arms… And I don't want to wait. Life is short and I don't want to waste another minute. Still, I know this has been one hell of a day. Maybe this isn't the best time to walk Lilah though our new life plan.

I follow Lilah, wrapped in a towel, to my bedroom. I stop short and laugh when I see the mattress on the floor. I completely forgot we broke the bed. We collapse on the mattress, because at this point, it's the best option. Lilah is crashing hard. I can see the exhaustion pulling her eyelids down. The adrenaline and shock have worn off and we both just need to sleep. Lilah curls up in my arms, her back pressed against me as I pull the blanket over us.

"Love you," she mumbles sleepily.

She can't see the grin her words bring to my face, but I kiss the top of
158

her head before smoothing her damp hair.

"I love you too," I whisper as I feel her body relax against me. I fight the drowsiness, listening to her breath and appreciating the feel of her.

***

I wake before Lilah, sneaking out of bed for some water. It's late afternoon and police cars still line the street, though the commotion has finally died down. The neighbors have gone home, now that there aren't any juicy details to witness. My car is still defunct in the driveway and crime scene tape flutters in the breeze.

"Fuck this," I mutter. No way are we staying here another night. Everything is broken or tainted by that little shit, Terrance. I grab my phone to make a couple calls but quickly realize those are going to have to wait because I have dozens of missed calls and messages from Lilah's family.

Maybe: Francine Donovan: This is Lilah's grandmother.

Olive Donovan: Our grandmother is freaking out. I told her Lilah needed to rest. Ignore her calls but have Lilah call when she's up to it. Please and thank you.

Donovan Automotive: This is Lukas. Can you have Lilah call me?

Maybe: Francine Donovan: I need to talk to Lilah, is she ok?

Maybe: Julia Donovan: Is this Ben? Lilah needs to get her ass over here. Gran is freaking out.

Maybe: Francine Donovan: Olive says Lilah was fine and that I'm being crazy.

Maybe: Francine Donovan: Fine, just call me when she wakes up.

Maybe: Francine Donovan: Is she up yet?

Olive Donovan: Seriously, Gran is fine.

I text them all back, letting them know Lilah is fine and still sleeping. I promise to have her call as soon as she wakes up.

Rubbing my hands together, I get to work. I make a few phone calls and call in a couple of favors. Maybe I can't fix everything while Lilah sleeps, but this much I can do.

***

It's nearly sunset by the time everything is in place and I am ready to get the hell out of here with her. They hauled away my massacred Jaguar an hour ago. In its spot sits our newly purchased Mercedes SUV, my bag and Frankie's stuff in the back. The dealer was all too happy to drop it off on short notice. Money will do that.

There's a soft knock on the door and when I open it, Olive steps inside with a grin.

"You're lucky we like you," she says by way of a greeting. "Gran wanted to storm the gates and take Lilah back to her house. We talked her down, but you two better be at the family dinner on time tomorrow night." She hands me a duffle bag. "Sally stocked her up and if I know Sally as well as I think I do, I'll just preemptively say 'you're welcome'."

I've heard enough Sally stories to be concerned. "Should I search it for illegal moonshine or Bon Jovi CDs?" I ask her with a grin.

160

Olive flips me off. "I can't believe Lilah told you about that," she huffs as she turns towards the door. "Have fun," she tosses over her shoulder. "And don't be late tomorrow or I'll send the boys to take Lilah back." I laugh out loud because they can try, but they'll have to pry her from my cold dead hands. "Or maybe we'll just let Gran have at you."

That's actually enough of a threat to make me stop laughing.

I open the door for Olive to leave but before she can take more than a couple steps, my curiosity gets the better of me. "Hey, was it you that put that invitation in my mailbox?"

Olive looks back with a mischievous smirk. "I have absolutely no idea what you're talking about," she says before turning away.

"Thank you!" I call out after her. She waves a hand over her shoulder and gets in her car.

I close the door, just in time to see Lilah walk out of the bedroom. She's wearing a t-shirt she must have found in one of my drawers because it comes halfway down her thighs. She rubs some sleep from her eyes and stretches, exposing a tempting amount of smooth leg. The worst part of me wants to drag her back to bed and hide out in there until her family comes busting down my front door looking for her.

"Was that my sister?" Lilah asks as she steps into me, wrapping her arms around my waist and pressing her warm cheek to my chest. I rub her back, enjoying the feeling of holding her like this.

"Yeah, she dropped off some clothes for you, but now that I've seen you in my shirt, I might just chuck the bag straight back into the street," I tease.

"You better not," she says, smacking me in the chest. I feign an injury, sending her into peals of laughter. God, I love it when she laughs like that.

She snatches the duffle bag and takes it to the bathroom. I follow her and lean on the doorjamb as I watch her dig through the bag.

"Where on earth did Olive get these?" she asks. It's hard to be sure, but from where I'm standing there seems to be an awful lot of lace in there. I suppress the urge to rub my hands together in glee.

161

"Sally," I tell her with a grin.

"Well that makes sense," she says as she yanks things out, one by one before looking up at me. "Put those dimples away, sir!" She shakes an adorable finger at me, making me smile harder.

"Why would I do that when I know how much you like them?" I ask her.

"Shameless," she mutters as she slips a pair of black silky panties up her legs, her hands disappearing under my t-shirt as she gets them situated. Shameless is right. I watch her hungrily, mentally calculating how long it's going to be until I can remove those with my teeth. Lilah is oblivious to her effect on me as she whips the shirt off and slips her arms through the straps of a black lace bra. "We should order you a new bed so we don't have to keep sleeping on the floor," she says as she reaches back to fasten the straps, thrusting her impressive rack my way.

My mouth goes dry, but I manage to respond. "Nah, it can wait. We're leaving."

Lilah's head whips up, a dress halfway up her arms. "What do you mean, leaving?" she asks.

"We are getting the hell out of this neighborhood. I got us a place down the road." I'm getting her away from all the crime scene tape and shitty memories of the last 24 hours. We can take the good ones with us.

Chapter 36: Lilah

"We can't just leave," I argue. I mean, we can. It's not like money is an issue, but it seems silly to rent a whole other house when we can just order a new bed. I finish pulling the dress over my head. True to Sally's opinion of how I should dress, it's about half a foot too short but looks amazing. I've been enjoying the way Ben watches me while I get dressed. I swear he almost choked on his own tongue when I stripped out of his shirt. The man is like a constant ego boost between the gawking and little whimper he made when I looked over my shoulder at the mirror, smoothing the dress over my butt.

He doesn't push back, just smacks me on the butt and leaves the room. "Trust me," he calls over his shoulder as he heads towards the kitchen. I pull my snarled hair into a messy bun. I need a real shower, one with conditioner, and a brush to fix this mess, but Ben seems determined to go. I shrug at my reflection. What the hell? I'm up for a mini vacation. Especially if I get more alone time with Ben. This place better have an amazing shower and a sturdy bed frame. Ooh. Maybe a hot tub...

When I join him in the kitchen, he hands me his phone. "You need to call your grandma from the road. Olive talked her down, but she's worried about you."

Oh my god, of course she is! I think, putting my hand over my mouth. "How could I be so self-centered?" I whisper, guilt clutching at my chest.

"Honestly, Princess," Ben says as he touches my cheek. "I think maybe you were in shock. You were pretty out of it until we got into the shower. And then you were distracted." He wiggles his eyebrows, making me laugh. "She'll understand. She knew where you were and that you were safe. Olive had her under control. Just call her."

Ben picks up Frankie's cage and my duffle bag full of illicit Sally goodies. If he had any idea how much lingerie was in there, I doubt we'd be leaving the house. When we step outside, I'm hit with a wave of nausea. There are still two police cruisers on the street. A light is on inside my house, the front door propped open. Crime scene tape is fluttering in the breeze and as I stand frozen, looking at my house, I understand why we're leaving. I look back at Ben and smile sadly at him. His cheek twitches, pulling his mouth to the side in a sympathetic way. He knew it would make me unhappy to see this and that man would do anything to protect me, even if it's just renting us another place to stay for a bit.

Ben holds out his hand and I take it, turning away from a house that I know I'll never live in again. I only have a second to be sad because as we head towards the driveway, I'm distracted by the huge black monstrosity parked in the Jaguar's spot.

"Jesus pleasus! Where did that thing come from?" I ask.

Ben laughs and opens the passenger side door for me. "The dealership," he replies with an adorable smirk. "They dropped it off while you were sleeping." He looks excessively smug about this.

I hop in, and he kisses me before closing the door. He sets Frankie's cage in the seat behind mine, strapping a seat belt around it, and my heart nearly explodes. My ovaries aren't far behind either.

We drive south; the sunset casting long shadows over the vineyards as we drive by. Ben holds my hand in his, his thumb drawing little circles over the back of my hand as I talk to Gran. She alternates between chiding me for not taking my brothers seriously and weeping, telling me how grateful she is that I'm ok. She threatens to come get me if we don't make family dinner tomorrow night, and when Ben grins, I'm willing to bet he's already been on the receiving end of these threats.

I hang up as we pull into a driveway. A wooded lot surrounds a gorgeous green A-frame house. It's lit up from inside and a car is in the driveway. I give Ben a questioning look as a middle-aged woman in a pantsuit steps out of the front door. He grins at me and jumps out of the car. She approaches us, her high heels wobbling in the gravel. She smiles pleasantly at me before holding a set of keys out to Ben.

"You must be Mr. Clark. Everything you requested is inside and the paperwork is on the counter." She smiles at me. "Have a lovely evening, Mrs. Clark."

164

I open my mouth to correct her, but she's already tottering away on her 4-inch stilettos and I'm afraid to break her concentration, lest she snap an ankle. Ben smirks at me, not at all bothered by the realtor confusing me for his wife.

"Come inside," he tells me as he grabs our bags. I unbuckle Frankie and follow him to the front door. I know there must be vineyards all around us, but this little house feels like it was plucked out of fairyland. Ben holds the front door open for me and as soon as I cross the threshold, I'm hit by the smell of Pad Thai. My stomach rumbles aggressively, reminding me that I've neglected it for far too long. Bags of takeout are perched on a coffee table in front of a giant squishy-looking leather couch. A bottle of champagne in an ice bucket and two glasses sit beside the bag.

Holy shit, this man gets me.

I set Frankie down and turn to kiss Ben, but he's on a knee in front of the door, our bags set aside. He has a ring box in his hand and the sight makes my breath catch in my chest. My hand goes to my mouth.

"Ben," I whisper. "When did you get that?"

He gives me the sweetest crooked smile I've ever seen and takes my hand in his. "That first morning I made you breakfast. You went to work, and I went ring shopping."

He clears his throat and straightens his glasses. "Lilah, I've loved you since I first laid eyes on you in that bar. I loved you covered in pickle juice. I loved you when you were drunk and chastising me in the middle of the night."

I laugh as a tear rolls down my cheek. His gaze is soft as he goes on, "I loved you with every touch, every kiss, and every word you spoke. The truth is, I didn't know I was living in the dark until you gave me your light. I'll love you for as long as I live. I want to spend my life with you. I want to raise little Ben and Lilah babies with you and let them make us both a little crazy. I want to wake up to your smile every morning for the rest of my life."

I'm such a baby. Tears are streaming down my face like tiny rivers breaking their banks.

"Lilah Donovan, will you marry me?" Ben's voice is rough with emotion when he asks, and I feel it through every inch of my body. I'll never forget that sentence for as long as I live.

"Yes, oh my god, yes," I laugh through my tears. Ben stands and holds me in his arms as he kisses me breathless. He stops long enough to slip the ring on my finger. I'll have to appreciate it later because right now all I want is for him to hold me. I wrap my arms around his neck and jump into his arms. My legs wrap around his hips as his lips meet mine. This man will catch me every time.

Epilogue – Lilah

Four months later

Julia cackles, head thrown back as Parker, the owner of Sorry, I'm Booked, reaches over and tops up her glass of wine, grinning at my sister's reaction. When the sign went up in the building across the street six months ago, Olive nearly exploded with glee. The romance-only bookstore seemed specifically designed to drain our bank accounts and supply us with unending amounts of smut, but the real win was meeting the proprietor, Parker.

She uses our coffee and places catering orders for her events, and in exchange, she hosts our monthly book club in her shop. Our book club may be a thinly veiled excuse to drink and talk about sex but it's my new favorite night. Mostly because being away from Ben for a couple hours gets both of us so worked up that he goes full Alpha on me afterwards. Tonight is going to be even better because I have a surprise for my possessive fiancé.

I reach into my purse and look at my phone, covertly texting Ben:

Me: Anytime now…

Ben: If you want to keep those panties in one piece you better take them off before I get there.

Heat spreads across my cheeks and my core clenches at the thought of Ben ripping my panties off of me. This is why I never wear the good stuff anymore. He can destroy as many pairs of cheap lace panties as he wants. I sigh out loud at the thought.

Olive squints at me and I pull my hand out of my purse, giving her an innocent expression. She smirks as she leans back in her chair, crossing her legs, taking a sip of wine and checking the time on her watch. Busted. I've started a countdown and Julia's going to be pissed when she finds out.

"…But why don't they just talk to each other?!" Julia yells at Chelsea. "It makes no sense! He's a grown-ass man. She's a grown-ass woman! Why does the entire story hinge on the fact that they're too chickenshit to say how they feel?"

"It's about vulnerability and overcoming their fear of rejection!" Chelsea argues back, tapping her hand on the book aggressively.

"Here we go," Olive mutters as Chelsea and Julia square off.

"I'm just saying, it's not realistic! He's all macho and Alpha on his motorcycle but-"

Parker is staring off out the window, her cherubic face dreamy as my sisters argue about this month's book, which was her pick. I have to say, I adore her. You'd never suspect someone who looks so innocent would sell such an impressive array of dirty books. Last month, I bought an entire series of filthy space westerns to read with Ben. I may have to keep his new-found love of romance novels a secret, but nothing turns me on like Ben reading a romance novel out loud while I lean against his chest, his voice vibrating through me… I shiver a little, shifting in my seat.

"Well, that's no excuse for his behavior! A hero has to be more than just be good in bed!" Julia argues as the bell over the door chimes, echoing through the shop as my very own hero wedges his broad shoulders through the small door frame, followed by a grinning Brooks, and a dejected-looking Lukas. Okay, I might feel a little bad that my text broke up their night out too. I know Lukas was really excited to hang out with Ben and Brooks, even if he would never admit it out loud.

"Are you fucking kidding me? Who caved?!" Julia asks, eyeing Olive and I exasperatedly.

Ben winks at me and my already pink cheeks ignite as desire pools somewhere much farther south. Julia doesn't miss the guilty expression on

168

my face, or the thumb Olive throws in my direction.

"Omg you are so weak!" Julia huffs. I throw back the last inch of seltzer in my cup and grab my purse. Julia borderline pouts as she smooths the hem of her dress but I'm more interested in Parker. She's eyeing my brother like he's the second coming of Christ bringing her a chocolate cake.

Lukas is slouched against the wall but the sulky expression he walked in here with has morphed into a smolder as he looks Parker up and down. It's adorable but also, because it's my brother, *yuck*. The two of them seem oblivious to the rest of the room and everyone watching them until Julia scoots her chair back, the feet screeching against the floor.

"I'm going to move before someone drools on me," she snarks as she gets to her feet. Parker's cheeks flush until they almost match her strawberry blonde hair.

"What?" she asks Julia, her eyes wide.

"Oh, nothing. I'm just going to leave the splash zone before things get icky."

Chelsea chokes on her wine and sputters. Far from looking ashamed of himself, Lukas is smirking at Parker and probably thinking thoughts that would make me yak. Oh, hell no. No way is he going to inflict his serial-dater ways on sweet Parker.

"OUT!" I bark, pointing at my little brother. He doesn't move until I get within poking distance, and even then, it's at a snail's pace. He winks over my head at Parker and pushes his back away from the wall, arms still folded across his chest. I know for a fact that he's trying to make his arms look as muscular as possible, so I smack him and push him out the door.

Ben follows me, trying, and failing, to muffle his laughter.

"Lukas, you leave Parker alone," I hiss, pointing at him as he climbs onto his motorcycle. He smooths his hair back and puts on his helmet. No way am

I letting him repeat the Sadie debacle. He broke my high school best friend's heart and she never spoke to me again.

"Calm your ass, Ladybug. She's not my type anyway," he says with a half-hearted shrug. He cranks up the bike and roars away into the night.

When we turn to leave, I see Parker standing behind us, her hazel eyes wide. Oh, shit. How much of that did she hear?

"Parker," say. "I'm so sorry. Lukas is a dick. He just says that kind of shit to rile people up."

She laughs, the tension easing from her eyes. "It's cool. For what it's worth, my daddy would hate him."

"I think most fathers would," I agree, laughing.

Parker grins at me and holds out my book. "Don't sweat it. You left this inside. Have a good night."

"Oh! Thank you! I can't believe I forgot that!" I give her a big hug before Ben and I head to the SUV. I've adjusted to the beast even though I tried to talk Ben into getting another Jaguar or something he would enjoy driving more. He adamantly refused, repeating that my safety was his top priority and, when he gave me that devilish grin with the dimples, I couldn't argue with his reasoning. I've been driving my Jeep but pretty soon I'll need something with a real back seat.

I give Ben a sly look and fiddle with my engagement ring. The diamond glints in the lights of the other headlights. The emeralds circling it look inky in this light but, as Ben points out, they match my eyes perfectly under sunlight. The ring is stupid big but I love it. No one would look at it and wonder if I'm single. Ben is progressive in so many ways but when he lays claim to me, he does it *right*. I squirm in my seat and lick my lips at the thought. Jesus, I can't wait to get home.

Ben gives me the side eye, lifting his eyebrow and grinning in a knowing way. "You okay over there, Princess?"

"Yes," I huff. "We live too far from downtown."

Ben gives me that cocky smile and slides his hand up my jean-clad thigh. The warm weight of it would be torture enough, but he gives my leg a squeeze before inching his hand between my legs, rubbing the seam. The rasping of the denim against my wet panties sets heat coursing through my body and my clit throbbing.

"Fuck," his voice rumbles through me. "You're so wet I can feel it through your jeans." My breath escapes on a moan and my hips roll against his hand. God, it feels so good. I want to rip my clothes off and ride his fingers. I reach for his lap, desperate to wrap my hand around his hard cock but he removes his hand, catching my wrist.

"No distracting the driver." His voice is low and even though he sounds like he's under control, the ticking muscle in his jaw gives him away. It only does that when he's furious or wildly turned on, and I *know* he's not angry. I smirk to myself as he releases my wrist and turns onto the long quiet street that leads to our rental. My hormones are raging but I still should have known that wouldn't work. Ben is nothing if not a stickler for my safety. Even so, I can't help teasing him. I lean my head back against the headrest and look at Ben as I run my hand up my leg. Slowly, I stroke my fingers over my thigh and up my stomach to cup my breast.

My fiancé eyes me darkly, his gaze darting between the road and my fingers as they dip into the front of my shirt. Ben shifts in his seat and growls under his breath as he pulls into the driveway. He brakes a little too hard, throwing the SUV into park. Ben cups the back of my neck and pulls me close. His eyes are fiery with lust and an absolutely filthy smirk pulls at the corner of his lips. That look is enough to tighten my nipples to aching peaks, my body electric with anticipation.

"Out, Princess," he growls.

I quirk an eyebrow and give him a teasing smile as I quip, "Yes, sir!"

Ben kisses me hard, his tongue sweeping into my mouth, claiming me with his passion. I grip his shirt, pulling him closer. His fingers work swiftly, unlatching my seatbelt and pushing it aside. He leans across my body, his chest scraping my sensitive nipples through layers of cursed clothing and I gasp against his lips as he throws my door open.

"Out." He sounds gruff but the wink he gives me is everything.

Ben is already halfway around the back when my feet hit the gravel drive and he's on me, his warm body caging me in. I lean back against the Mercedes, my hips pressed against the hard heat of his erection. Ben wastes no time going for the button on my jeans, yanking them to my ankles. He whips my shirt off over my head, dropping it to the ground as he draws my nipple into his mouth through the thin lace of my bra. I arch and moan into his hot mouth, arousal washing over me, blocking out everything except for his tongue and his fingers dipping to my core.

Ben's finger teases my clit with light taps before sliding lower and slipping through the wet arousal coating me. His moan vibrates through my nipple, electric need shooting straight to my clit. Ben plunges two fingers inside me, stroking and pressing the little bundle of nerves in exactly the right way. My legs shake, trapped by jeans as I reach for release. I've been dying for this, for Ben and his touch, for hours. My body needs it so badly, but he stops short and I cry out in frustration.

"Dammit, Ben!"

He grins like a sexy villain before picking me up and spinning me around. My hands hit the cold metal and glass of the car as he flicks the catch on my bra. My nipples, damp from his mouth, hit the cool night air, tightening to almost painful points. I arch my back as Ben grips my hip, holding me in place as he rubs the thick head of his cock against the slick lips of my pussy, grazing my clit and making me cry out.

172

He leans over me, the warmth of his chest covering my bare back and pressing my aching nipples to the unforgiving side of the Mercedes.

"I shouldn't reward your teasing, but your pussy is so wet. Tell me you're aching for it," he whispers gruffly into my ear. "Tell me you need this cock."

God, I love when he gets like this. "I'm aching for it," I moan, pressing my ass back to feel his heat at my core. "I'm so empty. I need you to fill my pussy up. I need your cock. Please fill me up."

Ben surges into me, impaling me bare. I gasp in pleasure, full to overflowing. He pulls back, thrusting into me over and over. The swell of his head rubs my G-spot with every roll of retreating pressure and answering plunge. His fingers grip the dip of my waist with one hand, the other reaching around to stroke me. His fingers glide through my juices, collecting the moisture and sliding along the side of my clit until I'm a panting, whimpering mess. My body is throbbing with my heartbeat, my need hovering, threatening to boil over until Ben grips my hair, pulling so he can see my face.

His deep eyes focus on mine and he growls out the words I love. "Come for me, Princess. I wanna feel it. I need to feel that tight pussy come."

I combust, tendrils of pleasure shooting through every nerve of my body as he groans into my ear. His fingers flex against me as his body jerks over mine, his release a frantic eruption.

He holds my trembling body as we both try to find our muscles.

"Thank god we don't have neighbors," I laugh into the night air. Ben kisses the top of my head, chuckling as he straightens up, sliding out of me with a little moan. We've been skipping birth control ever since we got engaged and I shamelessly love the feel of him bare. We both want kids and don't want to wait. We haven't been trying for a baby exactly, but we made the conscious decision to stop using birth control. The wildly uninhibited sex is a happy side effect.

"I'll keep us neighborless, even if I have to buy the entire valley," he promises. I bend down to pull up my jeans and snatch my shirt off the ground, making Ben groan at the view.

"You didn't get enough?" I giggle as I pull my jeans up and button them, euphoric after that orgasm. I turn to face him, still topless as I look for my bra.

"Never," Ben grins, all dimples as he pulls me to his chest. He cops a feel, playfully squeezing my breast. "Jesus, have your boobs gotten bigger?" he teases.

"You know, I think they have," I tell him with a grin. I've been waiting all night to tell him, and I can't hold back my glee any longer. I was trying to think of a clever way to do it, but this is close enough. He cocks his head to the side, his eyebrows drawn together. I can practically watch his brain spin as he thinks. His fingertips graze my belly button.

"Lilah, are you--? Did we…?" the hope in his eyes is almost too much to bear. I figured it would take ages to get pregnant, but I guess we got lucky.

"You're gonna be a daddy," I tell him with a grin.

Ben's eyes go wide, his handsome face equal parts joy and panic as his breath huffs out of him. He breathes hard and fast, sinking to the gravel driveway and putting his head between his knees, hyperventilating.

"Ben!" I laugh, rubbing his back as I pull my t-shirt on with one arm. "Are you okay?"

He gets his shit together *almost* as quickly as he lost it, but his eyes have a little shine to them as he looks up at me. His elbows rest on his knees and he looks so bemused. His palm is pressed to his mouth but there's no hiding the huge smile behind it.

174

"Happy?" I ask, even though I know the answer. Ben stands, a little shaky, but mostly back to normal. He pulls me into his arms, wrapping me in his warm embrace. He hugs me tight, kissing the top of my head.

"Ecstatic," he says with a little laugh. His breath ruffles my hair and my chest squeezes as I hug him back, loving the feel of his ribs expanding and contracting. In my heart, I know Ben will love me forever. There's nothing he wouldn't give to protect me and the little family we are going to make. This mountain of a man is my home and my other half, and we are going to be so insanely happy.

The End.

Keep reading for a note from the author and an excerpt from Revved Up, Lukas and Parker's book.

Author's note

Thank you so much for reading <u>Mowed Over</u>!

Listen, you need to know that I'm a total sap. I tear up at the drop of a hat and I'm deeply emotional about this little family. The outpouring of love and support I received after releasing <u>Stripped Down</u> was truly staggering and I can't tell you how grateful I am that you stuck with me through another book.

If you follow my newsletter, you might already know that I wrote Lilah's story before I wrote <u>Stripped Down</u>. It was all borne out of that scene where she falls out of bed and confronts a very smug, very shirtless Ben. As I worked on Lilah's story, Olive's character was screaming to go first. And once I thought about it, I realized that Lilah's story made more sense after she watched Olive fall in love. So, I switched gears, and I'm so happy I did!

When I came back to Lilah's book, I thought I'd just do a quick edit and be ready to publish in a few weeks.

Cue the emotional sobbing.

Lord was I wrong! In the course of writing Olive's book, Lilah morphed from a delicate, naive, wallflower into a strong and fiercely loyal goddess. Everything had to be rewritten, especially the dialogue with Ben and the sex. The sex was all wrong! In the end, I scrapped about 30 pages of sex, which now sits on my hard drive, getting the side-eye from all of my other works-in-progress. Even Ben got a makeover. (Makeunder?) He was originally this perfect, never-made-a-mistake-in-his-life kinda guy. Essentially, he was boring AF.

Terry. Honestly, I tried to write out the stalker and lean more towards the lighthearted feel of <u>Stripped Down</u>, but it never felt right. I have the Sonoma series plotted out with a story for each of the Donovan siblings. Some of them are funny and light while others are more emotional, and I think that for better or worse, these are real people in my head. Their stories are all different, but they share the journey together. I'm tearing up now just thinking about Asher's happily ever after! Told you I'm a sap!

Lukas is up next and, seriously, get some fresh panties for that one. I freaking love Lukas and Parker together. Julia and Asher both have their own stories coming up after Lukas. I don't want to give anything away, but I think you guys are going to love them.

If you have a minute to leave a review, it would mean the world to me! Just a quick rating with something like "I loved it!" is immensely helpful! Every review helps!

Thank you again for all your love and support!

Sincerely,

Mae Harden

P.S. I'd love to keep in touch with you! I'm usually pretty speedy to reply to messages on Facebook and Instagram, and you can always find me in my Facebook group, *Mae Harden's Happily Ever Afters*. I also have a mailing list where I host giveaways and send out occasional updates.

Let's keep in touch!

Facebook Group: Mae Harden's Happily Ever Afters

Facebook Page: Mae Harden Romance

Instagram: mae_harden_author

Other books by Mae Harden:

Stripped Down (Sonoma Series, Book 1)

Mowed Over (Sonoma Series, Book 2)

Revved Up (Sonoma Series, Book 3) - Coming December 2020!

An excerpt from Revved Up
by Mae Harden

Parker

I like bad boys. At least, I like them *in theory*. Growing up the chunky, glasses-wearing daughter of a pastor and a librarian, my experience with boys was limited to supervised dates with the closeted son of the assistant pastor. He was as much a bad boy as he was into me, which is to say, not at all.

But a girl can fantasize. And when I do, it's about a long-haired, tattoo-covered, tall, dark and handsome man on a motorcycle. He steals me away on the back of his hog, the engine rumbling between my thighs as we fly down the road, wind whipping through my hair--

"PARKER!"

I yelp and tumble backwards off my stool, landing hard on the wood floor.

"Oh my god! I'm so sorry!" Lilah yells as she rushes around the counter to help me.

"Ow," I moan, rubbing the back of my head as I sit up.

"Jesus, you're as clumsy as me," Lilah holds out a hand to help me up. I take it, letting her help me to my feet before brushing myself off. Not that the floors are dirty. I'm meticulous about keeping my little bookshop clean.

"You ok?" my friend asks with an apologetic grimace.

"Oh, I'm fine. Just a little bruised. You scared me!"

Lilah laughs, her green eyes full of mischief. "Dude, I said your name like three times! You were super spaced out. What were you thinkin' about?" She wiggles her eyebrows at me and I'm sure I blush.

She picks up the book I dropped on the counter, flipping it over to read the title. A shirtless man, all bulging muscles and long windswept hair graces the cover. A model-gorgeous woman sits behind him on a motorcycle, her arms draped all over him while he glowers into the distance. *Le sigh.*

"Didn't you finish this already? Book club is in two and a half hours," she asks, waving the book in my direction.

"Of course, I finished it! I've read it twice already. I was just flipping through it again before book club."

"Well that explains the thousand-yard stare," my friend laughs as she sets the book back on the counter. "God, this one was hot. You have good taste, and that's coming from someone who isn't even into the whole rugged-motorcycle-man thing."

She sets a bag on the counter next to my vintage typewriter. It doesn't work but it looks so good in the shop that I can't part with it. I peek inside the brown paper bag.

"Seltzer?" I ask her with a little frown.

"And wine. Don't get your panties in a twist, Parker," she laughs as she unloads the party supplies for tonight. "I got carried away with the Cabernet last weekend. I need a booze-free night tonight."

Pfft. Yeah, right. More like she's pregnant and not telling anyone yet. We've only been friends a couple of months but there's no way the Lilah I know is voluntarily giving up a glass of red wine.

"Okay," I say noncommittally as I try to keep my eyebrow from creeping up my face. I snag the little brown box stamped with the Olive Branch Bakery logo and crack the top, huffing the chocolate infused air and moaning.

181

Lilah laughs. "Don't get too excited. We're experimenting with new flavors and we need guinea pigs. There are some weird ones in there."

"I volunteer as tribute," I sigh, resisting the temptation to steal one of the shiny little truffles. I close the box and set it aside for later.

"You say that now but wait until you hit the rosemary caramel. It's… different." Lilah grins and hands me a salad in a takeout container with big toasty pieces of ciabatta on the side. "I know you don't have time to eat dinner between closing and book club."

"God, I love you!" I tell her, taking the salad and giving her a one-armed hug. I don't know what I would do without Lilah and Olive.

I moved to California on a whim four months ago. To date, it's the single boldest, bravest thing I've ever done. Sometimes I look around and I still can't believe I did it. I packed up my beat-up old Honda Civic and drove to California, all alone, with just enough savings to start my business and escape another dreary Minnesota winter and a town I can't stand.

When I stumbled across the rental listing for the little shop in downtown Sonoma, I just knew it was fate. I could feel the warm California sun on my skin and picture myself driving past miles and miles of picturesque vineyards. I could start fresh and be anyone I wanted to be.

Of course, in my fantasy I had a convertible and giant sunglasses and endless free time to explore wine country all by myself. The reality of opening a business is something else entirely. Long days stuck inside assembling bookshelves, painting, ordering books, organizing, cleaning, bills and never-ending paperwork.

I'm pretty sure I'd be miserably lonely if it wasn't for the sisters at the bakery across the road. One week after signing my lease, I put a sign up in my shop window reading:

Coming Soon!

Sorry, I'm Booked! – A Romance Bookstore for Everyone

Within minutes, Olive and Lilah were at my door, ready to break it down if I didn't let them in. That sums up my relationship with the Donovan sisters perfectly. Julia had arrived fifteen minutes later, breathless, and declaring "this better be worth" her break at the hospital. Spoiler alert, it was.

Lilah hugs me fiercely before heading back to the bakery. I spend the next two hours helping customers and tidying up the shop. I polish the wood counter, sweep up, and clean the fingerprints off the glass front door before locking up. I pull my salad out of the little fridge in the back with a happy sigh and settle in to read while I eat.

Book club is everything I ever hoped it would be. The three Donovan sisters and our friends, Chelsea and Sally, fill the eclectic collection of couches and chairs in the shop's sitting area. Chelsea and Julia heatedly debate the motorcycle romance I picked for this month's read while I top up wine glasses and straighten the cheeseboard Olive brought over.

"It's about vulnerability and overcoming their fear of rejection!" Chelsea all but yells. Judging by the way she's holding her copy of the book, I hope Julia has better catching reflexes than I do.

"I'm just saying, it's not realistic! He's all macho and Alpha on his motorcycle but he's such a pussy about speaking his mind!" Julia argues back.

I sigh to myself. I love this hero. He's all dirty talk in bed and fiercely possessive but Julia isn't wrong. He is a bit of a pussy when it comes to his feelings. The two of them keep arguing while Olive, Lilah, Sally, and I look on, eyes bouncing between them like it's a tennis match and grinning at each other. This happens every month and I think it boils down to the fact that

Julia and Chelsea are just inherently opposites. Chelsea is all sweet innocence. The blushing bride type living happily ever after with her Prince Charming.

Julia is loud, outspoken, spontaneous, and fearless. She is unapologetic about living her best life. I envy her. Moving out here is the only spontaneous thing I've ever done, and it was the best decision of my life. I've got my fresh start and I can be New Parker. Spontaneous Parker. Maybe even Wild Parker... well, probably not. I still have to manage the day-to-day bookstore stuff. It's not like I can go out and party every night. But I can be spontaneous.

The little brass bell over the shop door chimes, pulling me out of my thoughts. Ben, Lilah's fiancé enters through the narrow door, angling his shoulders to fit properly. He's almost frighteningly large in my opinion, but tiny Lilah adores him. Olive's fiancé, Brooks, follows Ben inside and a third man steps out from behind them, leaning against the door frame.

A tingle of electricity runs through my body, stopping my heart and my breath all in one go. Dark hair falls across part of his face, brushing his cheekbones and obscuring one of his eyes as he purses his lips in an irritated way. He doesn't look at all happy to be here but that doesn't stop my body from reacting with aching awareness.

Julia is yelling something about someone caving but she might as well be yelling into a bucket of water for all I'm picking up on it. I can't tear my eyes away from him. He's thick and muscular but not really chiseled.

Tattoos cover his arms, disappearing under the sleeves of his tight black t-shirt and trailing all the way down his wrists to the backs of his hands. I can even see some ink peeking out of the collar of his shirt. I wonder what they

184

look like and the thought of him lifting that shirt off over his head makes my mouth go dry.

There's something sweet about his face and I'm not sure what it is until he meets my eyes and a smirk lifts one corner of his lips. Holy god his lips are pretty. The pout was nice but that indolent little smile is staggering.

I'm staring.

I know I am.

But if I thought I couldn't look away before, it's nothing compared to the way I feel when his vibrant green eyes hold mine. Look away? I can't even breathe right. His eyes slowly sweep over my body, shameless and bold, and his eyebrow lifts in an appreciative way. I squeak. Like a little mouse.

Thankfully no one hears me because Julia is saying something about drool, scooting her chair back so that it screeches on the floor.

"What?" I ask her, ripping my eyes away from the man by the door. He has to be one of their brothers. The dark hair and bright green eyes are a dead giveaway and when my eyes finally land on Julia and her pouty lips, the family resemblance is unmistakable.

Julia gives me a rueful smile, eyebrow arched, as she says, "Oh, nothing. I'm just going to leave the splash zone before things get icky."

Chelsea spits wine down her front and I must look like a deer in the headlights because Julia's face softens towards me. I feel heat rise in my cheeks as my eyes dart from Julia back to Lukas. It's got to be Lukas with the tattoos. I've heard enough about their brothers to know Asher is too straightedge to have tattoos. Lukas is the troublemaker, at least that's what Olive says. And he sure as hell looks like trouble from where I'm standing.

His little smirk grows into a devastatingly lazy smile. He runs a hand over the shadow on his jaw and I'm the worst because all I can think are dirty thoughts. Best friend's brother or not, I wonder how that scruff would feel scraping my inner thighs. What would it be like to grip those muscular arms as he drove into me?

"Lukas! Out!" Lilah yells as she heads towards him, all but pushing him out the door. He lets her shepherd him out the door but not before giving me a wink. Ben follows them, a hand pressed to his mouth. And then everyone is staring at me, eyebrows raised, cocked, scrunched and lifted.

I feel my cheeks burn as I shrink into myself. I wish they would stop. Why can't they all look at something else? Talk about something else, *anything else* for Christ's sake. I spot Lilah's book on the coffee table, snatch it and follow her out the door. Anything to escape.

"Lukas, you leave Parker alone." Lilah's voice hits me as I step outside, but Ben's enormous frame is blocking her from my sight.

"Calm your ass, Ladybug. She's not my type anyway."

The deep, smokey voice hits me like a ton of bricks to the stomach. I feel like a fool. Everyone I know in California just witnessed me have a mental break at the sight of that man. They watched him look me up and down and deem me unworthy. That wink was just a parting shot.

I hear him start his motorcycle and drive off. A second later, Lilah turns and sees me, apologizing profusely for her brother.

I do my best to play it off, despite the sick pit in my stomach. "It's cool," I tell her with a smile I don't feel. "For what it's worth, my daddy would hate him."

That's not totally true. My dad doesn't *hate* anyone. He certainly wouldn't approve of me dating a man like that though. Not that it matters, since a man like that would never even consider someone like me. I give her my most convincing smile, even though I still feel cold inside, and hand her the book she forgot. Lilah and Ben leave, walking down the street, his arm wrapped around her protectively. I kind of just want to sit down and cry on the sidewalk but there's a crowd of people right inside my bookshop so I put on my best *everything-is-perfect* face, take a deep breath and head back inside.

Acknowledgements

Ok. I know I'm going to forget someone and feel like an asshole about it. I really do have a ton of people to thank for their support and for helping me get this book out into the world, if I've forgotten someone, I am so sorry!

I dedicated this book to my girlfriends, Emily, Becky, Brittany, and Stacey. I cannot thank them enough for keeping me sane, cheering me on, and still meeting my eye line after reading all the dirty bits. I don't know what I would do without you four.

I want to thank my beta reader, April Claudina, not just for catching little discrepancies, but for her suggestions on making my character's connections deeper. She also helped me with Stripped Down and I can wholeheartedly say my books wouldn't be the same without her.

My writing group, the RWSL. Holy mother of god, do I love you guys. Thank you for sharing the highs and lows, the frustrations and the laughs.

I specifically want to thank authors Juniper Kerry, Claire Hastings, and Celia Nott. I don't think I could do this without you three. Thank you for the emotional support, for bouncing ideas back and forth, for reading for me, catching my mistakes, and generally keeping my head on straight. Your friendship through this process has meant everything.

Thank you to my editor, Amy Maranville at Kraken Communications for polishing and perfecting my book baby. I'd be a hot mess without you.

I want to thank my family. My sisters, who read my books, and my parents and brothers who thankfully DON'T read my books. Their love and support means everything to me.

I want to thank my kids (who will never read this). It's not easy for them to give up mommy time when I need to work but they've been incredibly patient and sweet while I transition to a work-from-home career. I should probably also thank Paw Patrol for giving me an hour a day completely free of interruptions.

Last, but most importantly, I want to thank my amazing husband, who works his butt off all week and still takes charge of our kids so I can work through the weekend. He is the most loving and supportive man. I truly couldn't ask for a better partner to share my life with. All the best characteristics of my book heroes come straight from him. I love you so much.

With unending love and gratitude,

Mae Harden

About the author

Mae Harden is an author, pastry chef, podcast co-host, and lover of all things dirty. She writes contemporary romance with a penchant for dirty talk and a healthy dose of humor. Mae lives in Virginia with her husband and two kids, a chunky cat, and a pair of fluffy border collie sisters.

For more on Mae Harden and her work, visit her website:
www.MaeHarden.com

Manufactured by Amazon.ca
Bolton, ON

17233737R00116